Journey to the Stars

Science fiction stories from the bottom of the ocean to the depths of space

Christopher McMaster

Journey to the Stars

Science fiction stories from the bottom of the ocean to the depths of space

Christopher McMaster

Southern Skies Publications

ISBN: 978-0-473-57388-1 (Paperback)

978-0-473-57389-8 (Epub)

www. southernskiespublications.com

First Printing, 2021

For Ana, Tyler, Mohi, Riki, Driscoll, Harri, and Mara. May the seas you sail always be smooth.

Acknowledgements

'The Ethnographer's Gift' originally published in *Breach* #10, © 2019.

'Journey to the Stars' originally published in *Kaituhi Rawhiti: A Celebration of East Coast Writers*, © 2020.

'Stepping Out: The Personal Log of Captain Elizabeth Sheridan' originally published in *Revolutions*, © 2021.

Contents

Introduction

I have preferred the longer stroll of writing a novel. With a novel, I have to slow down, and let the story unfold in all its complexity. It takes time, and at times, that can feel like coaxing information out of a reluctant partner. I have to buy it another pint and ply it with questions, or be quiet and let it share. That's when the story begins to reveal itself, to tell itself. I've always enjoyed the long distance, whether running, hiking, cross-country skiing or sailing.

But writing these was fun. The stories in this book showed me (or reminded me) what a great vehicle the short story can be to explore and try to probe deeper into ideas or concepts. Like the 'death mind' in *The Ethnographer's Gift*, or shared consciousness in *Close Encounter*, or even time, like in *Earth Story* and *Twisted Love*. Short stories can also be a great way to test out an idea for a longer piece, something I might want to examine closer, and spend more time with, before I take it on that long run/hike/ski/sail of the novel. I've earmarked a couple of these stories to do just that.

The stories here are in no particular sequence. You can read from cover to cover, or dip in and out wherever you like. At the end of this collection there is a special section where I talk more about each story and the writing process. I consider it a 'conversation', because that is what I want it to be. It's a chance to explore the concepts or genesis behind each story, and even some directions they might lead in the future. It also lets you into the writer's mind, a look behind some of the decisions involved in creating character or place. You can save it for after you've read all the stories, or flick back after reading a story to learn more about it. I always enjoyed when authors offered that, and I hope you do too.

A few of the stories are from universes I created in my novels. *Stepping Out, The Originals,* and *Second Seed* are related to the *MisStep* novels (*MisStep* and *Seeders*), science fiction manuscripts being readied for publication. *Solo* explores the themes found in my *Lucid Series,* three books published by Dreaming Big Publications, (*American Dreamer, Tomorrow's History,* and *Gods and Dreamers*). All of these stories stand on their own. You don't have to read the novels, but I hope you might want to. At the very end of this book there is a section about those novels (the blurbs from the backs of the books). There is also a link to my website, so I hope to see you there!

Christopher McMaster

48 °48.78' S, 167 °36.38'E

(at the moment)

The Ethnographer's Gift

An alien ethnographer collects death moments for his study. One Autumn morning he starts to show Chloe ...

The man in the front of the car was angry, you could tell by the expression on his face. He was having trouble navigating through the dense traffic. He was late. He was thinking about trying to get there on time, that his wife would be angry, that he had a splitting headache. The children in the back seat weren't helping. They were shouting at each other. And at him.

"Give it back! That's my book!"

"I'm just looking at it!"

"Give it back! You always take my things without asking!"

"Ow! Dad, she hit me!"

"Both of you knock it off, I'm trying to drive!" Now the man was also shouting.

"Don't! You hurt me!" The man adjusted his rear-view mirror and could see hands flailing. He took one hand off the wheel and blindly reached back. He lifted it and slapped downward, catching one of his daughters on her knee. There was another "Ow!" from the back seat.

The man felt bad. He rarely, if ever, raised his hands to his girls. The car, in a situation like this, with all the pressure and all the risk, was one of those occasions. The stress of the drive was overpowering him. His mind was full of conflict, you could clearly see that in his expression. He wanted to be somewhere else. He was agitated. He was angry. He felt guilt for losing his temper.

The girls went quiet. Their anger at each other lingered. It sat between them like a sack of garbage polluting the back seat.

The father turned his head, just for a moment, to look at his girls. He saw them hurt, scowling, staring down at their knees. He wanted to see their eyes. To say, with a simple look, that he was sorry. He didn't see the truck travelling down a road on the right. The truck driver didn't see the red light. The sounds of metal meeting metal and the shattering of glass were deafening.

When the noise stopped the man and his daughters lay lifeless in the wreckage.

"Why are you showing me this?" Chloe asked. She was visibly upset by what she saw. She crossed her arms as if to give herself a reassuring hug.

"This is one of my favourites," she was answered. "Did you see the look on the girls' faces?"

"Yes, I did," Chloe said coldly. She didn't like what she watched. It worried and frightened her.

But her companion went on, sounding more excited. "They really loved each other very much. They were just like any family. They just got lost in the heat and the boredom."

"They're really dead now?" Chloe asked.

"Oh yes, they are," he answered. "I think they both knew they loved each other. Like the father. His expression, after he smacked his daughter, you saw that?"

"Yes. Yes, I did." Chloe, in fact, couldn't get it out of her mind. It was an angry look, but also soft and sad. His ...

"His last moment, what an amazing moment," Chloe's companion interrupted her thoughts.

"Here, take a look at this one," he continued. Chloe watched as he reached into a leather satchel and withdrew another glass-like ball. He could have lifted it with one hand but he used both with great care. He set it down on the table in front of her. It was opaque and smooth and round.

Chloe had just met this man. He spoke to her and sounded friendly. He seemed to have sensed her loneliness as she sat at the park table, hardly aware of others enjoying the fresh autumn sunshine. She wore her solitude like a comfortable coat, content to live more in what she had lost than where she was at the moment. Still, she found herself welcoming this stranger's intrusion. He was smiling as he approached, asked if he could join her. She found herself smiling in response and indicating to the empty bench. She couldn't quite remember his polite comments that broke the ice between them, but they somehow warmed her, somehow disarmed her.

Now she sat transfixed, gazing at the sphere the stranger had just placed on the table. She watched as the ball became clearer and shapes began to form.

The family woke in the middle of the night. Their subconscious, their dreaming selves, sensed something wasn't right. It couldn't identify what or why, but its cry was enough to wake them. The mother was first to realise what was amiss. She shook her husband roughly.

"Dan! Wake up! There's a fire in the house!"

Dan's eyes opened wide. He lay motionless for a moment until his sleeping mind joined his waking body. He saw the room was filled with smoke. His lungs hurt, his eyes watered.

"The kids!" he thought.

"Get up!" He shouted. "Get out of the house, I'll get the kids!"

He stumbled out of bed and rushed to the bedroom door. He put his hand against the wood to feel for heat before he slowly opened it. He found the hall full of smoke. It was very hot. There were flames below in the lounge. They would soon be climbing the stairs. He rushed to each of the three bedrooms, shouting into each room, "Get up, there's a fire! Get up! Come here!"

They would have to escape the house through the window at the end of the hall. His wife was already there. She had opened the window and was helping the first child, a boy of about six, through the window frame. It was a three metre drop to the ground, but it was the only way out. A second child, a girl, and slightly younger, came out and joined her mother. She was crying.

"Nick!" the father was shouting. "Nicolas!"

He turned to the girl. "Where is your brother Nick?" he demanded.

The girl looked at her father and continued to cry, speechless and too frightened to speak.

The fire was rapidly ascending to the first floor, drawn by the open window. The heat was becoming unbearable. Dan shouted again for Nick, but was answered only by the crackle of the fire. He shielded his face from the heat and entered a bedroom. His skin was blistering. He shouted again for his son, he tried to look in corners, to see through the heat and smoke, but had to retreat from the inferno. He ran, stumbling, coughing, down the hall, tripping and falling through the window.

Nick crouched trembling in the wardrobe. He couldn't see in the pitch-black darkness but his eyes were wide and scared. Every fibre in his being was trying to get away from the heat, the heat that grew worse every second. He tried to move to the left, then to the right. He pushed as deeply into the wardrobe as possible. He was screaming. He was crying. He was coughing, gasping for breath. The heat grew so intense his hair crinkled and singed. Finally, in a moment of agony that felt like an eternity, he passed out.

"Perhaps I shouldn't have shown you that one yet. It is very disturbing."

Chloe was crying softly as the images in the glass ball faded.

"It is very powerful, a very intense moment. He suffered greatly." The man Chloe had just met carefully took the glass ball and placed it back into his satchel. She heard it clack against others. Chloe looked at him now with a little fear in her eyes. She didn't even know his name. She was sitting at the park picnic table, minding her own business, and yet she welcomed his company. Now she was worried about all this death and pain he was showing her in his magical glass spheres.

"Are they real, the people in the balls?" Chloe asked.

"They were once," the man replied. "But what you watched were more like … memories. Like snapshots of a moment."

"Are they all the same type of moment?" Chloe meant of people dying. She was thinking all of this rather ghoulish.

"You mean of death, of the death moment. Yes, they are. It is very unique, very special." He seemed pleased somebody was interested and apparently unaware of Chloe's growing discomfort. An excitement was returning to his voice.

"Who are you?" Chloe asked.

"I am a researcher. I do field research. I study people. You might call me an anthropologist, or an ethnographer."

A small shiver ran through Chloe as she looked more closely at the man sitting across from her. She wanted to ask her question again. She searched for words to rephrase it. "You are not from here, are you?" she finally said.

"No, I am not," he answered slowly. He looked into the blue sky. "Were it dark now, I could perhaps point to a distant light." Then he remained silent.

He was forcing her to search for more words. There was a game of sorts going on now. He seemed to want to tell her something more. She wanted to know what it was, but didn't know how to ask.

"Why do you collect these moments?" she tried.

"What a wonderful question," he smiled. "These moments, they are so unique. It is the time when what you might call the spirit separates from the body, when the life that fills you leaves."

"But everything dies, what is so unique about that?"

"Where I come from it doesn't happen in quite the same way. Not the same way at all. And when a life is to leave, I am there, as if by instinct. My collections are actually very well known among my kind. What did you notice about each of the people in what I showed you?"

Chloe thought for a moment. "They didn't expect it or want it to happen,' she said.

"Exactly! In every life there is a moment, only one moment, when that life will leave its physical form. And in moment after moment, satchel after satchel, there is fear, regret, pain ..." his voice trailed off. It seemed tinged with sadness.

Chloe interrupted the silence that settled between them. "It sounds so terrible, so awful."

"Yes, it is. Sometimes terribly sad. My study is really of the mind, and what fills the mind in its last conscious moments. It is such an important moment, one that is inevitable, but feared. So many people know that they will die, and yet they refuse to face it. And when it happens, they are totally unprepared. Nobody thinks that *today* they might die, only it is always a *today* that they do."

Chloe was watching, listening.

"This time," the stranger went on, "it is my objective to collect a moment where the individual is aware that it is their death moment. No pain, or fear, or suffering, but acceptance."

As he finished speaking Chloe slowly got up from her seat. "I really must be going now," she said.

He smiled at her and replied softly, "it was a pleasure meeting you."

As Chloe walked away, she noticed, for the first time, other people at the park. Children were playing. The wind was blowing coloured leaves through the air. She thought of glass balls, of strangers, of pain and suffering. She thought of her own pain, of love lost. She travelled back in memory to cosy mornings in bed, the smell of her lover's hair, the feel of his body beside her. She felt her muscles relax, her body warm. *I might die today*, she thought, and found herself smiling for the first time in months.

She wasn't paying attention as she stepped into the street, but the driver of the car would never forget the look on her face before he ran into her. Looking into the eyes of the driver, in the moment before impact, Chloe turned her head and saw her death. Her expression was one of peace, almost of happiness.

Earth Story

With an asteroid hurtling towards the planet, a ship is sent to evacuate their colony. There are some who don't want to leave ...

It was magnificent, Tara decided, using the only word she could find that was appropriate. It was the most magnificent thing she had ever seen. She gazed up at the rocket. Its smooth surface reflected the light of the moon, painting the hull with silver. She craned her neck to try and see the windows near the cone where the pilots sat and controlled the ship. The stairs leading inside were down, and the entry door open. She could have climbed up and went inside, to look around as they were invited, but that could wait. She would enter soon enough.

"It's not bad for shuttle," a voice said.

Tara jumped, startled and a little embarrassed by the squeal she let escape.

"Sorry, I didn't mean to scare you," the voice said.

"You didn't scare me," Tara snapped.

She peered in the direction of the voice and saw one of the Homeworlders. He looked about her age, but as her eyes adjusted, she saw the cadet insignia on his shoulders, meaning he was perhaps a bit younger. Tara shook her head disapprovingly. Dark blue sash with gold braiding, an image of his ship, embroidered shoulder epaulet with even more gold braiding. They liked their costumes, these people.

She recognised him from the reception. If she were honest with her emotions, she was awed by the crowd, overwhelmed even. She had never seen so many strangers before. Through great effort she managed to keep her mouth from hanging open as she studied their uniforms, how they held their drinks and ate their food, and as the night progressed, even how they danced. Only when one of them tried to entice her onto the floor did she find it all too much and fled to the comfort of the night outside.

"Well, I am," the boy/young man/cadet said. "Scared. I'm just stumbling around out here trying not to bump into anything with teeth. How can you stand this darkness?"

"There is light enough," Tara answered, hearing the condescension in her own voice. She took a deep breath and exhaled slowly. None of this was his fault, even if he made a fine target. It was churlish to lash out.

"The night at home is filled with light," he went on, ignoring or not noticing her rudeness. "The star cluster fills the entire sky, not like this dim splash of light. Darkness and pinpoints of light, looking into the disc from the edge of the galaxy. We're so far from home!"

"I am home," Tara said.

"Well, not for long," the cadet said. "I'm Sarn. I crew on the ship."

"I can see," Tara said. "The uniform gives it away. Cadet?"

"Cadet First Class," Sarn said defensively. "I … I'm training to be an officer."

Tara felt her shoulders relax, as if a weight had been removed. She had been carrying a great deal, too much for a woman so young. She found her annoyance or anger at the Homeworlder not worth the effort, so on an unconscious level, set it down.

"I am Tara," she said, trying to be polite. The Homeworlder's ease made her self-conscious, feeling prim and old-fashioned, just like she felt ever since they arrived. "I am sure it must be very exciting," she added, looking up at the ship again and sounding prim and old-fashioned.

"You should have felt the thrusters coming down," he said. "She was really rocking as we burned through the atmosphere. But don't worry. It's always smoother going up, and we run a safe operation. And then you'll see the *Stellar Gem*. What a ship! Have you been topside?"

"Topside?"

"In orbit, above the planet, floating above it all."

"No," Tara answered.

"You're in for a treat then!" Sarn said, his excitement causing him to speak quickly. "She's an incredible planet. So much ocean, circling that huge continent. Beautiful green and blue, with white clouds swirling above it all. Oh, man," he added. "It's a shame she's going to be smashed."

Tara shifted her gaze away from the ship and towards Sarn. He was too young to read the subtle shift in her posture, and his eyes were unable in the faint light to see the corners of her mouth turn downwards. He ploughed on excitedly.

"That'd be something to see. An asteroid three kilometers across crashing into it. Bam!" he said, hitting his palm with a fist. "Dust clouds filling the sky, the crust so fractured volcanoes erupting everywhere, tidal waves hundreds of meters high! Acid rain. Acid fog. Imagine that! It's going to wipe everything out. The scientists on board want to stay and watch it. I mean, who wouldn't! But Captain won't stick around 'cause of the suicides. She says it'd be disrespectful, so we'll be well under way by the time it hits."

"What did you call them?" Tara asked.

"Call who?" Sarn asked.

"Those that are choosing to stay behind," Tara said slowly.

"Those that are … oh, the *suicides*," Sarn said. "What else can you call them? We're here to evacuate you, to save you, and they want to stay, knowing what's going to happen—"

"Don't call them that!" Tara said, picking up her anger again.

"What, the suicides?" Sarn asked.

"I told you not to call them that!" she shouted.

Sarn watched as Tara stomped off into the dark jungle. He scratched behind his ear, furrowed his brow and tried to think of what he may have said that made her storm off. Captain said these people may act unpredictably, that the crew must show respect. She said they might be—how did she put it? *Traumatised?*

Shaking his head, he followed the sound of music and returned to the reception.

Tara looked out over the field, watching the cynodonts graze. She smiled at the sight of their squat bodies, remembering what she asked her grandmother when she was just a youngling. It had become a family joke.

"Why do they look like they're always about to take a poo?" young Tara asked.

She couldn't recall her grandmother's answer. And she still thought they looked like they were about to defecate. Strong front shoulders at the end of long front legs, short hind legs and fat haunches— that was where the best cuts were, her grandmother often pointed out. She dreamed of farming them for their meat, breeding them in captivity, selling the steaks to the colony, even exporting off world. Grandfather would roll his eyes at the old woman explaining the same plan, going over new problems and solutions that would eventually fail. But her dream survived her husband, and she found another to tell it to, her granddaughter. It was easier than talking about more important things.

"I'm pretty sure with the new frequency they'll stay put," she said as she poured tea. "Buggers just don't like to stay put, even with the beautiful grazing land I give 'em."

She was talking about the sonic fence again. But Tara didn't want to change the subject or tune her out like in the past. She felt ashamed that she had ever done that, and wanted this moment to never end.

"The sonic fence?" Tara asked.

"You bet," she smiled. "They got that large head, but it ain't filled with much. I tried again last week. They just stand there in the sound wave, can't seem to move out of it, just stand there until whatever brains they have starts to melt out their ears. Lost three that way until I could turn the damn fence off. Meat locker is full, anyway. Couldn't just let them go to waste."

Tara let her grandmother's words fill her. They had the same familiarity as the constant drone of insects, the soundtrack of her life, and of everything else she knew and took comfort from. And soon it would be gone. She bit her lip, glanced at her grandmother, retreated into her tea cup, took a sip, and searched for the courage to ask one more time.

But her grandmother got in first, delaying the inevitable. "I know, the grain has been a success. It's that what fed the colony, and made the family prosper. But I always wanted to be a rancher. There's a special kind of pleasure working with the animals, even if they are dumb brutes."

"Is that Betsa down there?" Tara asked.

She peered over the railing at the cynodont Tara pointed at. The creature turned and pointed her black eyes in their direction, as if knowing she was talked about. Tara watched as the beast chewed, trying to remember what her grandmother told her was so special about an animal on this planet being able to eat and breathe at the same time.

"Now that one just won't leave," her grandmother said. "Her eggs hatch and those little ones just wander away, but not her. She ain't going anywhere, who knows why."

"Why won't you come with us, Grandmother?" Tara asked, finally finding the courage to bring it up. Again.

"Oh, Sweetums, we've been over this already," she said slowly.

"But Grandmother," Tara pleaded, "none of this will survive. The farm, the ranch, the cynodonts. Nothing."

"You are young, and starting over is for the young," she answered. It was not the first time she made that statement, but this time it was with more compassion towards her granddaughter and the pain she was feeling. "Even your parents are still young enough to start over. But I'm not young. I buried my parents here, your great grandparents. And they are buried next to their parents. It is fitting I am buried next to them."

"Come with us," Tara said. "You do not have to start again. We will do that. You can retire!"

"Retire! Can you imagine that?" her grandmother chided. She placed a hand on her forearm, looking into Tara's eyes. "Honey, stop it," she said gently. "I am staying. I am okay with that."

"But I'm not okay with that." It came out as a whimper, and it was all she could do to stop herself from crying.

Her grandmother squeezed her arm. "Tara, you will take with you memories, where I will always be, and even though it hurts, you will also take a strong heart, a heart that knows about loss, and thus knows how to love." She smiled at her granddaughter and got up from the table.

"I have something else for you to take," she said. She walked to a tall cupboard and removed a polished wooden box. Bringing it back to the table, she set it in front of Tara.

"What's in this box belongs to the family," she said. "I gift them to you, to gift to your granddaughter." Tara knew the contents. The sash and the crest badge inside were worn by her great-great matriarch upon landing on this world. She placed her hands on the lid and had no more words to stop her tears.

Tara checked herself in the mirror, the future matriarch of her clan. She adjusted the sash on her shoulder, straightening the tartan cloth for the umpteenth time. She touched the family crest, pinned where the sash passed over her chest. She removed the lid of the jar containing the lotion her mother made from plants in their own garden, and gave to her for this occasion. She dipped two fingers into the jar and rubbed the lotion onto her arms, and then her hips and legs, taking her time despite time being limited.

When she was satisfied with the sheen of her scales, she joined her parents, and together they made their way to the waiting rocket.

Journey to the Stars

A man's dream of meeting the lights he has seen in the sky, of journeying with them, turns to nightmare when he finally gets what he wants ...

Tom chased aliens like others chased storms. He chased them for the same reasons too. He met a group once, or rather, their paths crossed. Wild eyes and messy hair, they were more excited the closer they got to their storm. They obviously lived for it. He wasn't all that different from them—he was just as excited, just as wild-eyed, just as crazed the closer he got. On that occasion, he watched them peel away as the storm continued to move. They didn't understand why Tom didn't follow as the storm tracked west, but he wasn't interested in any terrestrial meteorological event. He was after what, or who, was hiding behind it. He *knew* something was there.

Just like the storm chasers followed their leads, Tom followed his. There were lots of leads to pick up on. Short wave radio was his favourite. It was awash in theorists, or conspiracists, and chasers like himself. And it was immediate. There was no delay in uploading files, no hours wasted in trolling websites or following endless paths with keywords for breadcrumbs. Tom prided himself in reading between the lines, in seeing relevant data in observations that the person on air didn't even see. He was also adept at picking out the plants, the hoaxers, paid by the government or whoever, to redirect the gaze, to sow some confusion. There was that place in America, what they called 'Area 51'. Now there *was* a conspiracy, just not the one a lot of people believed. Classic redirection. Simple, but effective. If you get people looking in one place, they aren't looking where they should.

Tom didn't care who paid them, the plants and hoaxers, or why they did it. He ignored their noise and listened for … *authentic* leads. It was that kind of information that led to meeting the storm chasers. He caught a few adjectives in a broadcast, a few geographical descriptors, headed to where he thought was mentioned, talked to a few locals. Hearsay is usually like gold dust, leading to a richer vein. He drove into the outback, lied to the storm freaks, and flanked the cloud bank they were following.

He saw them that time, if only a glimpse. The lights. Coordinated, intelligent lights.

By that time, he was already down the rabbit hole. He sold whatever belongings he had, quit his dead-end job, traded his rudderless life for a rugged old Ford with a camper shell over the bed and a shortwave radio. Stocked with water, a camp stove, a couple boxes of two-minute noodles and a sleeping bag, he was self-sufficient. Whenever a promising lead cropped up, he chased it. He could relocate to the new hotspot, triangulate his data, and be there. Waiting.

He waited on this night. He drove the Ford as far he could and left it parked by a ravine. He hiked through the gully, across more desert, and climbed a hill, the highest point in the vicinity. He looked to the north. All his data pointed north. And he waited, studying the night sky. He saw Orion reach up and across the expanse. In the New Mexican night sky, Orion stands upright, a warrior with outstretched arms. Tom had trekked their outback, a young pilgrim learning his trade. He left that place disillusioned with his guides, but much more skilled. Orion floated above him tonight on the other side of the planet, upside-down, diving into the distant horizon.

Hours passed. He waited. Tom was good at waiting. Then he saw them, lights in the distance. Five bright lights, moving in unison, then breaking formation and darting randomly over the outback, before re-joining the others. Tom watched as the group of lights moved towards him. He opened his rucksack and took out the set of road flares he had just for this occasion. He removed the caps, struck the lighter buttons and tossed them in a circle around him.

The lights broke formation again, scattered seemingly randomly over the outback, and rejoined. Then a single light broke away and moved towards the hill on which Tom stood. There was no doubt left in Tom's mind, it was moving towards him. He spread his feet in anticipation. He raised his arms in expectation. As the light neared, Tom could see its spherical shape clearly. It came to a halt directly above him, hovering silently. Tom looked up and saw light emerge from within as a panel opened. A beam of bright light surrounded him, bathing him in its glow. He glanced at his feet and saw that he was levitating off the ground, rising towards the light. Tom looked up, grinning.

It's finally happening! he thought. *Is this what joy feels like? Ecstasy?*

Tom entered the panel and found himself inside a spherical room that gleamed like stainless steel. He tried to lower his arms but found he could not. All he was able to move were his eyes. Movement in both sides of his peripheral vision caused him to shift his gaze nervously from left to right. He watched as small panels opened in the sides of the sphere. From each opening a mechanical arm folded out, folded again, and yet again, each time reaching closer to him. The arms folded a final time, and from the corners of Tom's darting eyes he saw at the end of each appendage a sharp blade. Tom breathed in, shuddering.

The arms moved and the blades flashed. Tom's clothing fell from his body. He looked down at his bare chest, his belly, his exposed penis. Even his feet were bare, his thick leather hiking boots lying in pieces beneath him.

A door in front of him opened and he floated through it. He was in another spherical gleaming room, only in the centre was a table. Before he reached the table, a panel opened in the wall and another mechanical arm extended, folded open, folded open again, ending with a nozzle that hovered directly in front of his face. Tom blinked as a cold liquid sprayed him, moving over his entire torso, waist, legs, and then the back of his body. Soon the feeling of cold faded, as did any physical sensation at all. He watched the wall rotate as his body was turned until he floated horizontally. He only realised he was lying on the table when he saw its edges out of the corner of an eye.

Movement caught his attention and he tried to see, willing his head to turn, but it refused to obey. He strained his eyes, stretching his optical muscles. He forced his eyes to remain fixed on the movement to the side of his body. An arm unfolded, unfolded again, and unfolded once more until a glistening blade extended. He forced his eyes in the other direction, to a movement there, and watched as another arm unfolded and unfolded until it ended in a small tray. At the same time yet another arm unfolded from the wall, ending in a pair of tongs. He looked back at the blade. It made a quick dip, and returned to its position, but now it was wet and glistening red. He flicked his eyes back to the tongs and watched as his nose was gently placed on the small tray. The tray retracted into the wall and was replaced by another.

Tom tried to scream but couldn't. He tried to move, to struggle, to resist. But his body would not respond. His panicked eyes darted from the left to the right. Every time the arm with the blade moved, he watched as another body part was laid on a tray. His lips. His tongue. The skin of his face. The blade worked its way down his body. He saw his nipples gingerly placed on a tray, one at a time, and watched as that tray retracted into the wall to be replaced by yet another. He saw the now stained blade move and watched as his genitals were deposited on a tray. The blade continued to move and his intestines were piled on a larger flat metal surface. Then his innards moved away from him, disappearing into a wall.

The knife flashed, the tongs pulled, and his kidneys were carefully lifted and deposited on another. Then his liver. Then his lungs. His eyes grew wide as his heart, still beating, was removed from his chest, placed on a tray and taken away. A blur blinded one eye, and with the one remaining he watched it placed gently on a tray, the eye looking back at him as it, too, entered a small panel in the wall.

Tom's remaining eye flicked rapidly left and right, up and down, as he tried to make sense of his surroundings. But those were far beyond the comprehension of his shattering mind.

He was the centrepiece of the exhibit, the climax of the experience. If he could see down the corridor, he would know what happened to all those parts of himself that he watched being removed. Mounted and preserved, they were a living exhibit. The largest of all organs, the skin, stretched to its full height. The internal organs. The muscular system. The vascular system … that filled an entire panel. Then there was the reproductive system. And, in a place of honour, was the crowning piece of the exhibit: the skull housing a brain kept alive through nutrient fluid and electrical impulse. The spinal column, hanging from the base of the brain, twitched, as if communicating to legs and feet that were no longer there. As if it were trying to escape.

But it was the eye that they came to see, flicking from left to right, and up and down, appearing wide and full of terror due to the absence of any skin, and definitely possessed of life. It rested within its socket, still connected by muscle and nerve. The eye could never see the label below it, and if it could, the being behind it would not be able to read the alien script.

It consisted of a simple description:

Planet Earth. Human, the label read. *Mature Male*.

The Locker Room

A platoon on a spaceship readies themselves for drops into combat in a space in between boredom and war ...

"Give me your data, Mohi. There's nobody in the quadrant you could reach," Tyler said.

"My mother's on Luna," Mohi said.

"Gimme your access code, man!" Tyler's voice took on a familiar shrillness. "You aren't gonna facetime her."

"Nothing's for free, soldier." I stuck an oar in because it was entertaining.

"Fuck to do with you?" she shot back. Tyler added a withering look to accompany it.

"Sell it if you aren't using it, Mohi," I tried again. She watched where my words went. Mohi wavered between the two of us, stuck in one of those social interactions he had little skill with. He had to be on a spectrum or something. You could see the cogs in his head trying to work out if he was being fucked with, or if it was serious. He understood violence better. A gun only had two ends, which was simple enough for him.

"Riki's paying twenty credits an hour for mine," I lied. We were allocated a small daily amount, rationed like water and just as essential for survival. Any contact with the outside gave nourishment. "Do I hear twenty-two?" Driscoll was wearing that grin I started to recognise as humour.

"Twenty-two, at least, Mohi," I added, ignoring Tyler's glare. "Twenty-two, going once, going—"

"Fuck out of it, Tio!" she growled. I hate being called uncle, but I guess I was, compared to her. She was younger than my daughters would be if they were still alive.

"Give me your code, Mohi. You're not using it!" She used that tone that made me glad I worked behind the safe end of her gun. I also saw a flash of the playground bully she probably was as a kid.

"Don't let her bully you, Mohi."

"Fuck out of it!" she hissed at me. Shifting speeds deftly, she added in the other direction, "Come on comrade, help the team."

I rolled my eyes for Driscoll's benefit as Mohi flipped her his access code. Tyler stomped out of the room, face already looking at her screen.

"She's going to make somebody a fine wife one day," I said.

Riki laughed, and turned towards the corridor Tyler removed herself to. "Hey Tyler, the old guy says you're going to be a good wife to somebody," he shouted out the hatch. He leaned towards it to catch her response.

"What'd she say?" I asked.

"I don't know," Riki said. "Something with 'F' in it."

I inserted an arm into my armoured glove and made a fist, raised it to my face and peered down the glistening barrels located above each knuckle. A duster in each hand gave out a mighty one-two. Not many got up after that kind of punch. Ana, our platoon leader, told me I was a 'southpaw', leading with my left to keep the right in reserve. She said it was a rookie thing, depending too much on the rocket launcher on that shoulder. If you need to use that in a fist fight, you're already fucked. Balance it out. It wasn't said as an order, or a critique, but it was both, given as a simple comment. I learned very quickly to take that kind of thing as order and critique, and make sure I went in two fisted on the next drop.

She was saying something now. I tilted my head in her direction. "Huh?"

"Tyler saw you go up to the bridge," she repeated.

I raised my eyebrows and added a smirk. "So?"

I *was* called to the bridge. The First Mate stopped by the armoury where I was polishing my shit.

Cleaning and maintenance between drops. Take care of your gear and it will take care of you.

"Captain wants to see you," he said. Brief message.

I told him I'd be right up, and kept cleaning. Sarge said clean it between drops, so that's what I was doing. I didn't understand how things worked yet, or whose boot kicked hardest.

"Why are you still here?" he asked.

It was a question with one answer. His boot was bigger. I set down the back plate I was working on, got up from the bench and made my way aft. The bridge was the opposite of the locker room. A plush leather sofa lined one wall, sound-reducing carpet covered the decking, computer arrays formed a semi-circle around half of the room, an espresso machine sat in the corner. An espresso machine, for Christ's sake. My mouth started to water.

I stood in the doorway, stiffly at attention. "Sir!" I saluted, waiting with my hand angled in front of my face. The captain crisply returned the salute and I lowered my hand.

"Please, take a seat," she said, indicating the sofa.

I sat, trying not to sigh out loud as I sank into the comfort. She took a seat from a nearby station. The officer sitting on it stood as she reached towards it, then continued working standing, ignoring the scene beside him. Captain sat and faced me.

"We've received a report from Earth defenses. There was a strike. I'm only telling you this because Laredo was among the targets."

Targets. Plural. That sounded bad. My mind shifted into a higher gear, trying to deduce why she was telling me this.

"How bad?" I asked to gain more time.

"The report lists the strike as catastrophic," she answered. "There is a window in comms should you wish to try to contact any family. You are welcome to access the system. Lieutenant O'Brien will assist you." She turned her head to point to a young woman sitting at a console.

That was it. I had told them when I signed on that I was from Tamaulipas, that my family lived in Laredo. It was easy to create a past when so much had been erased. They were worried about morale, so shit was bad. The espresso machine teased me from the corner of my eye. Fresh coffee. I swallowed. I could try the sympathy card to get a cup, but … no, it wasn't going to happen.

"Thank you, sir," I said.

I got up and went to O'Brien's station. She plugged in my device and I tried a few contacts that no longer existed. O'Brien looked genuinely sorry for me when I gave up after three attempts. I put on a suitably distraught face and left.

"What?" I called to Ana. Gearing up was in final stages, armour being secured, weapons checked. Lots of noise.

"Tyler saw you go into the bridge," she repeated. "She thinks you're a spy."

"A spy for who?" I asked. We're almost shouting just to be heard.

"I don't know," she answered. "The captain. Intelligence. Black opps. *Them*."

I stood up, flexed my arms, tested the knees. "Yeah," I said before closing my face plate. "Tell her one of those."

Tyler clomped by, a metal suit studded with lethal weapons. Driscoll patted his helmet, walked over and stood behind her, the tall Tongan making her look like a child. She almost was. I took my place beside the hatch, Mohi behind me. Harri joined the rear, so quiet you hardly noticed him, but always having your back. The non-coms took their places, Mara, the hardened vet that acted a mother hen to the squad when not in combat, and Riki in front of Tyler. Sarge walked between our short rows to stand in front of the door, waiting for it to cycle open into the descent shuttle, drop box, death cube, hell ride, whatever you wanted to call it.

The hatch seal hissed. She didn't have to say it, but she always did as she herded us in.

"Saddle up, cowgirls."

Drop—Smash—Withdrawal. Drop—Smash—Withdrawal. Repeat. Repeat. Repeat. We didn't ask about objectives or reasons in this cluster fuck of a war. We just did what we were ordered. The fewer the questions the better. I liked being the buck private. Bottom of the totem pole. Just do what I'm told, try to be competent, and stay alive. There was a very attractive simplicity in that. But I was lucky to have a good sergeant to serve under. She saw weak spots before they could manifest and re-allocate fire power where it was needed. She didn't bark or bite—she didn't need to. Just a quiet instruction, which meant do it, or I will do more than bite. *Use your right in the next fight.* She didn't have to tell me twice. *You're always the last in the locker room.* That was Driscoll's cop. It didn't escape any of our notice, the big islander sauntering in late. Sarge had a quiet word, now he was always on time, if not early.

Mohi sat next to me, leg twitching. He probably didn't even notice. As if *they* weren't enough, I'd need to keep a corner of my eye on him. "You gotta slow down, man," I told him after the last drop. "You move too fast, and you're going to get somebody hurt." I let that sink in, or at least try to, but I could see it just bobbed around on the surface.

"Somebody else, like me," I clarified. "I don't care about you. Or them," I added, gesturing to the others. "I care about me. Getting hurt."

His leg was twitching away, boot clacking on the deck, tap tap tap tap tap audible even through my helmet. I placed my gloved hand on his knee and it stopped. Shuttle detach any second now.

"Let's go fuck them up, buddy!" I shouted, but he couldn't hear through faceplates and the sudden lurch as we fell towards another drop zone.

Conversations every voyage start with leave-based exploits involving vast quantities of alcohol, an assortment of strippers, and the military police. Riki leaned over and spoke quietly during prep. Maybe I reminded him of his uncle, or priest. I don't know.

"I gotta knock it off, man," he said. "It'll kill me faster than *they* will. I always say it's the straight and narrow next leave, but it just sucks me back in." And then he proceeded to describe this particularly voluptuous redhead prostitute he spent all his pay on. During a drop he's called the Freezerman. Over two metres of muscle and guns, with deadly focus and titanium strength discipline. He's saved our asses more than once. I avoid him on leave.

Once the subject of drink wears off, topics begin to broaden. I see how far I can take them. Religion. Psychedelics. Economics. Dreams.

"Have you ever had a dream where you were awake in your dream?" I asked. We were kitted up, ready to drop, but the drop zone changed, buying us some wait time.

"Where you say to yourself, hey, I'm in a dream."
I am just fishing, seeing who might bite.

"I had a dream I was a woman," Mohi said. All
eyes are on him and the room goes quiet. "And I
was in bed being fucked by my brother."

"Shit man!" Tyler yelled. "Fuck away from me!"
she slammed her face plate down, encasing herself
in her armour carapace.

Ana is staring at me, wondering what my story
really is. *You don't belong here*, her look says. *But
here I am,* my look responds. That's the thing
about this job. On the drop it doesn't matter, but in
the locker room folks only know what you tell
them. Everybody has a story, but all the others
know is what you, or they, decide to say.

Ana tilts her head to the left, listening to a comm
line I'm not privy to. But I know what she is going
to say before she stands, walks to the hatch, and
says it.

"Saddle up, cowgirls."

Landing Party

Can we trust eyes? Our senses? Our feelings? How do we know what we experience is real, or just what somebody, or something, wants us think? Six astronauts might find out too late ...

"You'll have to call it soon," Wren said.

"I know," Sharp replied without taking his eyes off the view screen. "How can I lose the entire away team?"

"Anything could have happened."

Both the captain and mate stared at the barren world below. Another survey revealed no sign of the first landing party, no readings of communication systems, no sign of the landing craft or any evidence of debris. It was as if the planet had simply swallowed them up.

"Fourth away team has returned," Wren added. "There was no sign of Marby's team."

"I have their report," Sharp replied. Two weeks since Marby and her team descended for a survey of the planet. Routine. Collect samples, take readings. Boots on the ground, carry out their work and return. Their supplies could only sustain them for four days. The air on the surface was breathable, for a short time, but would poison them if they continued to breathe it. Once their own oxygen supplies ran out, there was no way they could survive long. It was a short and simple mission, designed and supplied appropriately.

Only on the descent, Marby reported a slight course deviation. She called in to allay any fears from those monitoring from above, and said new landing coordinates would follow. But then they disappeared. Only silence. All contact ceased. It was if the landing craft simply fell off the system, or out of existence. Three teams followed during the ensuing days in an attempt to locate the lost craft, and each found absolutely nothing.

You'll have to call it soon, he could hear Wren thinking, wanting to say it to his captain, again.

"I'll call it. Soon. Just not yet," Sharp said. "We can give them a little more time, at least." Though he knew they were out of time.

Marby was first out of the landing craft. She stepped onto the surface and took in the view. It was not what she was briefed to expect. She chinned the controls in her helmet and changed the screen displayed on her faceplate to infra-red. The readings confirmed her visual. She checked atmospheric readings, and then checked them again. She held up a palm towards Anderson, who waited in the landing craft airlock, to stop him from descending the steps to the surface.

She expected to see a barren windswept landscape. Instead, she saw soft green covered hills, and a light blue coloured the sky, not sand and stone under a burnt sienna dome. She checked the reading again. They confirmed what her eyes were telling her, right down to the level of nitrogen in what seemed to be a very breathable atmosphere.

Marby lifted her face plate. She tentatively breathed in through her nose. The air entered, cool and fresh. She breathed out, and breathed in deeper. There was a scent in the air she couldn't identify, but it was pleasant. She motioned Anderson and the others to join her. They formed a semi-circle around her. She smiled at their helmeted faces.

"It's okay," she said. "I thought the readings were all wrong, but they're not." She pointed at her open helmet. "Breathable. Earth like. Not toxic at all."

The others didn't move. Marby could see the doubt in their faces.

"It's not killing me," she said. She reached up and un-clasped her helmet, took it off and set it beside the stairs. Her bulky atmosphere suit suddenly felt heavy and extremely unecessary, so she took off her gloves and started to un-zip her suit.

"Ma'am," Anderson asked, "are you sure this is all right?"

Marby showed him her hands, opening both in a shrug that was lost in her bulky suit. "Yes, I am," she said with a sudden certainty. She stepped over and placed a hand on Anderson's shoulder.

"It's all right," she said, smiling at him.

Marby finished unzipping her suit and stepped out of it. On impulse, she reached down and took the stockings off her feet and let her toes wiggle into the mossy ground. She smiled as she watched the others open their face plates and begin to peel off their heavy suits. White helped Ariapa off with her boots, and seeing Marby barefoot, they took off their stockings as well. Ariapa had a beautiful smile. Marby found it amazing that she had not really noticed that before. Wenck and Afeti stood facing each other, their suits piled to the side. Afeti had his hand on Wenck's chest, looking up into the taller man's eyes. The under suits hugged the body, highlighting every muscle and every curve. Both men looked beautiful.

Marby felt a warmth inside, a sensation she typically tried to ignore or suppress, especially on duty. She let it warm her belly as she watched her team, and then she let it inch its way downward. She looked at Anderson, still in his suit, and wearing a slight scowl. She went to him and touched his arm, leaving her hand there.

"Can you smell that?" she asked. "I can't quite name it, but it is almost familiar."

He breathed in deep and exhaled slowly. The creases on his brow softened. He seemed to have set down a weight that he had carried off the landing craft. Doubt, or distrust.

"Cinnamon," he said. Marby saw a hint of a smile on his face. "But something else …"

"Let me help you with this," she said, and undid the clasps of his helmet, and then the zip of his suit.

When he stepped out of it, Marby sighed. He was exquisite. She tried to resist touching him, but was helpless. Her hand tingled as it came into contact with his chest. She felt him recoil, ever so slightly, ever so briefly, until a moment later it was forgotten. He smiled at her and his own hand raised and gripped her upper arm. He squeezed her strong muscles. She knew he felt it now, the warmth and the urgency.

"Take your socks off," she said. "Let your feet feel the surface."

He did as he was told. Marby watched the man's smile grow as his pink toes wriggled into the moss. The heat descending from her tummy grew lower and began to burn. A fleeting thought of ripping off his under suit flew too fast for her catch, yet lingered a short distance away, teasing.

She felt a pull and turned away from her crew. "This way," she said, and not waiting for the others to follow she walked away. But they did follow, in pairs. Anderson hurried to catch up with

Marby. He took her hand and they walked together. Cresting a small hill, they stopped. Below them lay a flat clearing, carpeted in soft moss. A small stream flowed at the edge, sunlight reflecting in the clear surface.

Marby felt Anderson's hand pull back slightly. A barely perceptible wrinkle formed on his brow. She knew the look he took when he tried to remember a lost detail or fragment of data, or when he tried to solve a difficult problem. She didn't want him to worry, or remember whatever he was trying to remember. She knew only that she wanted him.

She kissed him. Her lips touched his, and he responded without hesitation. Her mouth opened, inviting his tongue, which entered willingly. She pressed against him and felt his hardness against her belly. His hand gripped her breast, squeezing, and he pulled her closer.

Just as quickly, Marby pushed him away. "Come, over here," she gasped, and led him by the hand to the clearing by the stream.

She wrestled out of her under suit and stood before him naked. He pulled at his own and soon had it off, and then pulled her down on top of him. He slid into her easily and she gripped him with her thighs. She rose and fell, and rose and fell. The others followed them to the small clearing, and their example. She planted her hands on Anderson's chest as she rose and fell, and let out a moan that turned into a growl. Marby felt Anderson building towards climax, sensing him edge ever closer to the summit of his ecstasy, burning with the same urgency as she. Marby stopped moving and placed a hand firmly on his chest.

"No," she commanded, not knowing where the words came from. "Hold it, channel it. Feel our energy. Let it build. Move it through me. Take my energy. Let it flow, keep it flowing. It is so powerful. Feel it. *Feed us.*"

She moved up his shaft and slowly down, again, and again, feeling her own energy build, from the base of her spine to the top of her head. Her panting grew deeper, more audible, a primitive song to accompany their primitive dance. When she felt her whole body begin to glow, she rolled off him. She looked at her crew. White was on top of Ariapa, her legs wrapped around his back. Afeti held Wenck from behind, both moving in rhythm. On hands and knees she crawled towards them. She ran a hand down White's sweat covered back. She took his head in her hands and kissed him, pulling him off Ariapa and onto her. She felt him enter her and swayed with him.

"Breathe the energy," she heard herself whisper hoarsely into his ear. "Use it, guide it, *feed us.*"

Beside them bodies moved and joined, broke apart and re-joined in new combinations. Marby looked at the man above her and saw it was now Afeti, his beautiful black skin glistening. She smiled deeply, feeling the throbbing of his member and the pulse of his glow surging through her, mingling with her own, until they were one light, one glowing ball, seeping into the ground beneath them. Then she felt Wenck behind her, thrusting. And then Ariapa, rubbing and swaying and moaning.

Finally, Marby was spent. She let her head fall back and rest on the mossy surface beneath them. She breathed out a long and quavering breath. She tilted her head to see the others and grew cold. The moss they lay on was gone, replaced by alien dust and rock. Afeti lay nearby with Ariapa, but his beautiful body was emaciated, covered in bruises. His eyes were opened, but there was no life inhabiting them.

Marby quickly closed her eyes. When she opened them again, she saw the beautiful Anderson lying beside her. She nestled her face against his. She tried to smell him, to taste the cinnamon and … something else. She tried to feel the energy that burned so intensely, grasping for it, clinging to the memory. But instead, she felt emptied and wasted. She took a shuddering breath, wincing as it burned her throat. She smelled Anderson again, and pushed away from the stink of death. Her eyes moved from his corpse to where she lay. She felt rocks dig into her back and legs, fine sand pricking exposed and torn skin. The sun baked her as it did the world around her, a sun too close, a flame in a dirty sky.

She gasped, and the air scratched as it filled and poisoned her lungs. She heard only the wheezy shallow rasp of her own breathing as she lay on the barren soil waiting to die.

QMS

Fishing in the near future: New Zealand has one of the most sustainably managed fisheries in the world. What happens when those elsewhere fish their waters to depletion and start to head south?

Skipper got carried away so I was dancing in front of the weigh station, keeping loose as the fillets dropped into the tray waiting below. This part of the factory was like a video game with consequences. Get it wrong and there'd be hell to pay, the foreman biting my ear off or teammates helping me focus after shift. Nothing like a team that starts bitching. Or worse, docked pay. If I could spare any mental activity for computation, I could figure out how much each tray was earning the ship, the crew, and more importantly, myself. That would also help me stay focussed, seeing each tray as extra coin in my pocket. But I didn't dare take my eyes or mind off the trays and the scales they sat on. When the scale read seven point five, I punched the black stopper. Even before the door closed the flow of fillets, I shifted the tray to the packing conveyor, put an empty tray on the scale, stuck on the right coloured tab—red, yellow, or black, according to size, and opened the door to let the backed-up fillets drop down.

When all three trays hit their limit at the same time, now that was fun. I cursed the foreman for setting the speed of the conveyor. She expected everyone to run at one pace—hers. It was an impossible ask. She worked the trimming line, sorting each fillet by weight, cutting off any missed skin or bone. But I'd try, hands flashing, trays shifting, even doing a little footwork like a boxer in the ring just to annoy Tarryn at her weigh station, get her to look over, lose her flow. She never did. I glanced at the speed lever above me, tempted to move it slower, but I'd probably miss a tray.

It was a hell of a haul, at least forty tonnes. Skipper couldn't resist. It was a good season, the hoki were running, and there was money to be made. Lots of money. Enough to make me try to keep up with the foreman, hands flashing, trays shifting. Hit the stopper, move the tray, replace the tray, fix on a coloured tab. Yellow, red or black. The pace meant time would fly, because the mind was focussed. But it was still going to be a tiring shift processing this much fish, even with time on the wing. The deckies might come down and help after they tied the net down or set it for another haul, but I'd be dancing in front of trays for hours. The packers would still be laying fillets into boxes, trying to keep up with me, trying to keep up with the foreman, trying to keep up with *Schlosen 221*.

The *Schlosen*. A marvel of butchering ingenuity that took a whole fish, cut off its head and tail, sliced it in half, disposed of its guts and shaved its flesh into the thin pieces of meat the world was hungering for. There were three of them arranged in the factory, and each were purring as they sliced and diced. They still required a human to put the fish in the right way, to sort out the by-catch, drive the ship, set the net. Deckies were still up top. And I was still below. Maybe fishing hadn't changed that much, after all. It just got a lot more efficient.

The scale with a tray on it marked with a red tab registered seven point six and I deftly hit the stopper, moved trays, and placed an empty on the scale. As it began to refill, I heard the alarm. Four long blasts, followed by a pause, followed by four long blasts, the pattern repeating again and again. Over the hum of machinery and blare of music, it still hurt my ears. It was meant to. That bell was for me. I hit the stopper above the tray with a black label, moved the full tray to the packing line, replaced it with an empty. I tore off a black tab and stuck it to the new tray, my mind forcing my body not to leave the station, to wait until I was relieved. The golden rule, at least one of them. Never leave a station until relieved.

Finally, after what felt like hours but probably just a few seconds, I felt a hand touch my shoulder. I was halfway to the sink and ripping off my gloves before my heart completed a beat. I watched my apron fall on the deck after I missed the hook, ran my hands under a stream of water, and bolted up the stairs leading out of the factory deck and into the changing room. I grabbed a pfd, fastened it, and stepped through the hatch leading to the deck. The pfd was decoration, a tradition meant to make you feel safe. If I was in the water, I was dead, period, and no personal floatation device was going to bring me back because I was probably in several pieces. I patted the toggle at the left side, the one I'd pull if I was somehow, miraculously, alive. That toggle would activate the gas cylinder inside and fill the life vest with air. It helped a little, reassuring in a pathetic way. At least something was on my side.

I slowed my pace as I neared the speed boat. I passed our observer and slapped him on the shoulder, hard enough to make him stagger, hard enough to wonder if it was encouragement or something else. Government still looking over our shoulders. His job was to monitor and report, to watch while we harvested the nation's wealth. He counted the fish we hauled, watched as we worked, tested the size and sex of the fish, took biological samples to send back to the real scientists. His data helped set the quotas, those mysterious numbers we were given each year telling us how much we were allowed to catch and where.

"Watch this!" I shouted as I passed.

I guess his work played a role in this somehow. At least the government joined the team. At the beginning of the century the New Zealand navy had two frigates and a few patrol boats. Now it had about four times that, heavily armed and tasked with protecting the EEZ, or as we call it, *The Eazy*. The first E in that acronym is 'exclusive', meaning ours. While some fished their stocks to oblivion, we managed ours. Put a quota on stock, researched it, let the cowboys go out of business and sell their boats. Give the market what it wanted and pocket the profit. As fish stocks died out elsewhere because they didn't bother with a quota management system, ours got more valuable. Only, as other fisheries died out our waters started to look mighty attractive to other fleets. First, they encroached, shouting insults, cutting nets, ramming ships. Then they packed guns, which meant we did too. Vessels were boarded, holds emptied. Fishers killed. By the time the navy started actually acting like a navy we already had Pac-men and Droners on board.

Not that I could see warships nearby right now. This fight was going to be ours alone.

Manu, our spotter, was attaching himself to the bow. Rake grabbed her pulser and sat behind him. Toby, the bosun, handed me my skimmer and I climbed aboard, clipping on to the tether at my position. This was the bosun's boat, and as second mate he had something to prove. It meant he drove us and drilled us, but that's why I was here, my primary role. A Pac-Man. I don't know where the name comes from, some kind of old school game or something, an old deckie told me. That didn't matter. Patrol and attack. That was the Pac part. I was the man. High risk, high pay, and as far from the factory as you could get. I was here to defend our fish more than gut or weigh them.

I grabbed the side of the speed boat with my free hand as the crane lowered us over the side of the ship. Toby had the engine at full rev as soon as we hit the water. I focussed on my skimmer as we shot over the water, smashing through the waves. I opened the chamber and checked the missile inside was secure. It was a water line killer, punching a hole at the water line of the target vessel so large that nothing could stop the water. The missile flew so low it looked like it skimmed across the surface to its target. Turning behind me I nodded to Emma, my loader, as she prepared the second missile. Two shadows flew quickly over us, our Droners going to work, sending out their deadly little pests.

"Identity!" Toby shouted over the din of the outboard and thump of the hull. "Who the hell is out there?"

Manu peered through his sighting lens, trying to keep level as the speed boat bounced over the swell. Two flashes off our starboard beam meant our Droners were doing their job, keeping the eyes of our mystery guest busy elsewhere. Both were hit, but others would follow.

"Identity!" Toby shouted again. His voice was getting shrill like it usually did when he was excited.

I needed to know who it was too. If it was Chinese, I shot across the bow. A warning. A gentle way to tell them that they had strayed into our backyard, and would they kindly rectify what must have been an unwitting error of navigation and leave our exclusive economic zone. Sometimes my skimmer could be polite. There was some irony in that. Their insatiable appetite for fish depleted their own stocks and gave us enough money to build the ships needed to protect ours from them. But politics was politics, so we'd play nice and try not to start a fight with our most important customer.

Now, if it was Thai, I aimed at that red line Lord Plimsoll invented way back when to stop ship owners from overloading their vessels and becoming 'coffin ships' as they sank to the bottom and brought their owners rich insurance pay-outs. The red line was the limit of the ship that could be submerged for the vessel to navigate safely. It made a wonderful target. I magnified my sites, searching for the line to send whatever fishers on board to the bottom of the sea in their coffin. They could have flown our flags, played by our rules, hosted our observers, but they chose to steal instead. They didn't play nice, so we didn't play nice either.

"Drone approaching, two o'clock!" Manu shouted.

"Rake—"

"I'm on it!" she barked at the bosun.

"Take it out!" Toby shouted at her.

"Wait … for … it …" she growled.

The dark speck in the air grew larger as it tried to lock target on us. Rake moved her pulser to the right and then left to keep aim as Toby zigged and zagged. It was a race between its operator and our Pulser. After what seemed like minutes but was probably just a second or two, she jerked back as she fired, an electro-magnetic pulse travelling at almost nine tenths the speed of light leaving her weapon and hitting the drone, killing all its power. Rake dropped the empty magazine and replaced it with the full charge her loader handed her as the dead drone fell into the sea.

"Identity!" the bosun shouted. He was screaming like a little girl, no offence to little girls.

"Silhouette emerging," Manu said.

"That's not what I asked for!"

We should have detected the ship hours ago. It should never have gotten this close to us, or our fishing grounds. There were rumours of radar reflecting paint. The bitch floating out there must be covered in it. God knows who spotted her, but as soon as I find out I'm buying them a beer. If it was missed and night fell, we would have been boarded, our hold raided and our mutilated bodies tossed into the drink.

"I know this ship!" Manu shouted. "It's the *Bhangphu*! It has to be!"

We all knew that ship. The *Bhangphu*, a pirate Thai factory deep-sea trawler, eighty-two meters in length with a crew of sixty-six. Sneaking into our *Eazy* to harvest our fish before slinking back outside the zone and selling their catch. It didn't just take our fish, it took our future, it took our livelihoods. It was a tick sucking our blood, a leech, a vampire, pick whatever analogy makes you the angriest. It was growing fat on our hard work and sacrifice. I tensed my shoulders, bracing a thigh against the side of the speed boat, the skimmer at my shoulder steady and unmoving as the boat swerved and bounced.

"It's the *Bhangphu*!" Manu shouted again. "No doubt about it!"

I launched the missile, its exhaust plume streaking across the surface of the sea. Muscle memory took over as I opened the chamber and held the launcher at my side. Emma slapped a second missile in the chamber, which I closed and again aimed at the *Bhangphu*. I didn't have to fire it, but I did. A ball of fire filled my scope as the Thai vessel was torn open. I followed the second missile with my bare eye as Emma loaded a third into my weapon. Another explosion, closer to the bow, right where I wanted it. Toby slowed the boat and we all watched as the ship leaned onto its port, pointed bow down, and slid into the waves. We bobbed silently on the swell until the *Bhangphu's* stern disappeared beneath the waves.

Toby ended the moment by revving the outboard and turning the speed boat back towards our ship. He probably wanted to strut around the deck as soon as he could, while we all stowed our weapons and went back to the factory to continue processing the catch. There was really no need to rush back for that. It was nice out in the fresh air, and those fish would still be waiting.

Solo

Who will catch the killer, when the killer is from a different reality? It takes a dreamer to stop a dreamer ...

I found him sitting on a stool in the corner of a run-down bar. Real ambiance for the alcoholic, but he wasn't one of those. He was just pretending, like he did with the rest of his life, at least the waking part. I didn't give a shit what he did here, whether he was a drunk, a garbageman, a bagger at a grocery store, or that asshole at the DMV you had to deal with when you renewed your license.

He was the last one, by the way. He actually worked at the Department of Motor fucking Vehicles. But that wasn't why I was going to kill him.

He couldn't see me from where I was standing. I'd wait to introduce myself. Pretending to be a drunk sitting at a bar meant he had to drink, so I'd wait until he had at least two, maybe starting his third.

If need be, like if he nursed those two too slowly, I'd buy him that third. He'd take it as well, because he was that type of guy. This was the first real look I'd had of him. Most of what I caught were just glances, or following him from a distance, so far back that he'd never suspect someone was tailing him. I knew the back of his head, the shape of his body, how he walked.

I saw more of what he left behind, after he had finished and was no longer around. That was, literally, the stuff of nightmares.

The bartender looked at me, trying to decide what he was seeing. I gave him a warm smile to sew a little confusion and buy some time. He turned back to his bar and poured a drink for a real alcoholic sitting farther up. I had to be careful with my costume. Even this place didn't want whores inside hassling their Johns, and it was the girls on the corner I modelled myself on. A few changes should be enough to pull it off. Tight jeans with a glittery belt around my waist instead of very short shorts or a mini skirt. A blouse tight enough to show off my tits without revealing too much of them through a thread bare halter top, or a piece of coloured elastic they called a 'tube top' in this time and place. And flat soled shoes rather than heels. I could have probably worn all that other shit and made it work by avoiding the heels, and especially knee-high boots, but why risk it?

It seemed to have worked as the bartender ignored me after he poured the booze hound his drink and went back to whatever he did when pretending to work. He could polish glasses with a rag for all I cared, just as long as he paid me no mind and let me gaze uninterrupted at Mr Wonderful perched on his barstool. His moustache and wide collared shirt gave away the decade. The cheap wood panelling and neon of the establishment was another obvious clue. Only the seventies could produce such tacky décor, and that was in multiple realities. This one had its advantages. A woman in sexy jeans could stare across a low-lit tacky bar at a guy on a bar stool and not be thrown out. Or worse. Here she could even sit next to the guy, buy him a drink, seduce him into leaving with her. That was the plan, anyway.

Sure, he'd first think I was a hooker and guard his wallet, but that third drink would loosen him up enough to see what was on offer was willing and free. He'd even start to believe the lies I told him about his looks or his wit. Stroke his ego, massage it a little, give it a caress. It's not that he's stupid— he might not be, and I seriously doubt he is. And it's not that he's just a man and men usually fall for that kind of shit. It's that he thinks he's safe. That he's home. That nobody knows, or even suspects, what he really is or what he has done, because, quite simply, nobody does. Nobody can. And I look nothing like his type, his usual target. He likes them young and scared, in modest dresses. Not tight sexy jeans.

The thing is, he doesn't even know what he is, because he tells himself it isn't real. But what makes me touch the blade in my hand bag is that I don't believe it. I know he knows that's just a lie he tells himself. And that makes the next part easier.

I walked to the bar, sat on a stool, and waited. It was all about timing. You could only stand around so long until it became suspicious. I lifted a finger without looking at the bartender. He showed up a moment later and I ordered a bourbon on the rocks. I wasn't there to drink, but that didn't mean I couldn't. I was at a bar. It was a prerequisite for attendance. He set the glass in front of me and I listened for the ice to crack, smiled as it popped, lifted the drink and took a sip. One of life's little pleasures, awake or asleep. I slowly set the glass down and closed my eyes. I turned my face towards the end of the bar and opened them. He was looking right at me. I smiled, pretending to be shy, and looked down at my drink.

I like bourbon. I like the smell, I like the sound of the ice, I like the taste. There's no need to be an ascetic in this work. I'll take another sip, wait, take another, then shoot a furtive glance back down the bar and find him looking right back at me. He may be a monster, but he's also a man. Just like a trout in a mountain stream, with the fly dropping in the water, once, twice, three times, cast and lift, cast and lift … well, he would take the bait and get hooked. Next cast would be difficult. I could show no revulsion or hatred, no recognition, merely a coy glance and nothing more. He would sense anything else.

There is a street in another reality. Not really a street, more a narrow lane paved in cobbles, lined with terraced houses. They are so close that you can almost touch the buildings on the other side of the lane with outstretched arms. Almost. It is barely wide enough for a horse and cart. The second floor of these houses jut out and cover a couple feet of the lane. At night it is like walking down a damp, dark cave. Not many walk about at night. Especially the young women. That's how I learned about him, though at that time I didn't know who it was. I just felt the fear in the people, especially the young women. They didn't even want to talk about it, but in the end they did.

There was a beast lurking in the shadows. That's what they called him in whispered voices. *The Beast*. So most stayed in at night, while the monster hunted outside. Sometimes, however, it can't be avoided. You have to get home after work. You spent too long with your lover and didn't notice the sun setting and night fall. You have to deliver a meal to your sick grandmother. You refuse to be frightened of the dark and the monsters that lurk in the shadows. Whatever the reason or rationale, you make that fatal mistake.

The result is the same, for the unlucky. He hides in a doorway as she passes, and then jumps on her. He wraps his hands around her neck and squeezes so tightly no air or sound can escape. Her eyes bulge and her face reddens. She tries to resist, but he is behind her and his grip is strong. She is too frightened to think. She flails her hands, trying to rid her back of this predator. She tries to pry loose the hands around her throat. But by this time, she is too weakened by fear and asphyxia. Her vision darkens. Her legs grow weak. Her consciousness flickers and goes out.

When he feels her go limp, he adjusts his grip and lifts her in his arms, carrying her down to a narrower alley, takes her further into the gloom and like a bridegroom carrying his bride, he lays her gently on the ground. Then the bridegroom analogy becomes literal. He doesn't like them awake. For the sense of power, he places his hands back around her neck as he finishes, and to make sure she doesn't join him, that her eyes do not flicker open and meet his. Maybe that is his nightmare—being seen.

My nightmare is what he leaves behind. Below her waist, she is untouched in any other way. He wants everybody to know what a man he is. He positions her legs wide apart, knees bent. There is no mistaking what took place. Above her waist is different. He has carefully sliced along her throat, from ear to ear. Beside his work, placed with care, he always leaves his knife, cleaned from a cut piece of his victim's clothing.

I don't know why he does that. In a future reality those investigating serial killers will refer to it as a 'calling card'. A signature of sorts. Drawing a symbol, leaving a memento, even the way they cut. In one reality another killer's signature was how he mutilated his victims. They called that beast 'Jack'. After five gruesome murders, he apparently vanished. They had no idea how many others may have been cut by that madman in other times or places. There were many. But for them, it was enough to believe he was gone, whoever, or whatever, he was. I could tell them what happened to Jack, if I wanted to, and if I thought they wanted to know. I could even describe the look in his eyes when he realised that he was bleeding profusely from a sharp knife cut made by the blade in my hand.

But they don't want to know his fate. It's enough for them to know he is gone.

Calling cards. Signatures. Splayed legs, a slit throat, and a cleaned knife. Sometimes calling cards led to capturing the monster. Most of the time it didn't, and never would, because the killers have simply disappeared. Those that kill in their own realities can write their cryptic notes or leave their souvenirs. That type of psychopath, the one that kills while awake, scares the hell out me, if I'm honest. Thankfully, there's enough chasing them already, constables or cops, police or detectives, in those realities. Now, those that just disappear … that's what this particular beast does. He finds a quiet and dark place, slows his breathing and his heart, and wakes up. Somebody has to track *them* down, and it sure isn't going to be Sherlock Holmes. He wouldn't know what to do with the clues of this case.

I lift my glass, breathe in the rich earthy scent of the bourbon, lift it to my mouth, and sip. It flows across my tongue and I let it linger before swallowing. I lick my lips, furtively glance down the bar and briefly make eye contact. He is not used to women looking back, but he is off guard, because he doesn't know how dark this particular alley is. In another few minutes I'll get up and sit next to him, maybe leave a barstool between us. He'll see my glass is almost empty and offer to buy me another. If he doesn't do that, I'll help him and tell him to. I watch as he takes another drink from his glass. His second is almost empty. It is time.

"God has left us," one girl whispers.

"Do not blaspheme," her companion hisses.

They are terrified and traumatised. This is a result he never pays attention to, though he preys on it.

"He is a devil," the first continues. "He just walked into the shadows as if they are a door back into hell."

The shadows are a door, but not into hell.

I waited until the corpse of his latest victim was removed, after the place was blessed or protected by the priest, after everybody had left. I lit my candle and examined the scene. A large stain of blood marked where she died. I scanned an arc of cobbles leading away from the spot, holding my candle close to the ground. I moved from right to left, slowly, attentively, one yard away, then two. And then I saw the first of his prints, an inky spot on the cobbles. Almost another yard forward was another, and another. He stood in her blood, and carried it where he went. The prints led me to a dark corner, where they stopped, two bloody footprints. I used the candle to search forward, to look for more prints, but there are no more. They seem to simply disappear into an invisible door.

I looked at the buildings around me and saw a soft light. A curtain moved. I was being watched. I went to the house the light belonged to and knocked. There was no answer, but I knew somebody was inside. I knocked again, but softly.

"Is anybody there?" I asked, three simple words telling them I am female, I am harmless, I am like you.

"Please," I added.

I heard movement behind the door, whispered voices, a quiet argument. Finally, the door cracked open, they see me, and the door opened wider, swallowing me whole. I stood in their home, relieved and humbled. They were terrified, and yet they still give shelter and succour.

"You must not be out at this time!" I am chastised.

"Thank you," I said meekly, and they led me to a small hearth where a fire burned dimly. They sat me down as if I were made of explosives. I told them I lost my way, that I saw the stains on the stones, that I grew frightened. Finally, they decided to trust me and speak.

"God has left us," one girl whispered.

"Do not blaspheme," her companion hissed.

"He is a devil," the first continued. "He just walked into the shadows as if they are a door back into hell."

Her face drained of blood as she told what she saw. A man, or a devil in the form of man. Covered in blood, his hands and arms stained red, walking nonchalantly up the ally, stopping beside a wall, standing there for a moment, and then simply fading into nothingness.

"What do you mean, fading into nothingness?" I asked.

"He … it … I could see a man, even in the dark, and it … his body became lighter—"

"Lighter?"

"I was able to see through it. Not at first, but more and more, until it looked as mist or fog. Then he was gone. Completely gone!" She started to sob and was comforted by the other.

It is the confirmation I sought. I do not press them farther than they can bear. I take a cup of warm soup from them, thank them, and accept their offer of shelter for the night. When they wake in the morning I will be long gone. When I am certain they are asleep I creep out of their home and stand in the alley where the blood stains end. I empty my mind of thoughts, except for one, an intention, a focus, on the man who made those bloody marks on the stones and where he opened his eyes. Where he woke up.

I closed my eyes and thought of that place. I saw the black curtain in my mind that was left once the light was removed, and I stepped behind it. If there was a witness watching, they would have seen my body become lighter, until it looked as mist or fog, and then completely disappear. When the dark begins to clear, I see more shadows, until my eyes adjust to the gloom of an alley across from a tacky bar, where nobody notices a woman mysteriously appearing out of thin air.

I am tempted to order another drink. I really need it. I am tempted to wake up, to close my eyes and open them to familiar light. Not shadows or dark curtains, and what lurks in and behind them. This is a godless place.

But that is why I am here. There are no gods. Or they simply do not care.

Psychologists say dreams are the psyche's way to communicate with itself. They are a way for the subconscious mind to tell the conscious mind what it does not know and what it does not understand. Dreams are spontaneous manifestations of the unconscious. Dreams do not deceive; they do not lie. They are as simple or as complicated as the dreamer themselves. Dreams are individual. We need to understand what they are expressing through their imagery and symbols in order to understand ourselves, et cetera, et cetera.

Some of that might be true. We all dream, even if we don't remember every single one. And dreams serve a purpose. Sometimes. They can help cleanse our subconscious or inner mind. Like parasites burrowing to the surface of our skin, inner traumas or confusions or worries, through dreams, they surface and we let them go. Maybe, at times. I'll give them that much. But sticking to that kind of thinking is just a form of masturbation. Self-obsessing, self-analysing, narcissistic … to think that it was all about you and your problems or fears or neurosis! That's just wanking.

I think of dreams more as a multi-layered, multiversal energy that contains us all. And existence is energy, and like life, wants to continue. This energy feeds off other forms of energy, just like all life on earth feeds on other forms of life. We consume the living to continue living. Everything on the planet, even trees sucking up the nutrients of past life from the soil where they root. What people refer to as 'gods' do the same, only the energy that nurtures them comes through belief. To continue to exist, they need us to worship or fear or honour. They need our energy. They use us to shape realities, to push events in certain ways, so they can continue to feed on worship or fear or honour.

And I learned I wasn't the only person awake in my dreams. It is not too hard to wake up in a dream, to be aware that you are the dreamer, and realizing that what is around you in the dream is real, at least for those that call it their reality. Try it. Go to sleep with the intention of waking up in your dream. Usually, the awareness that they are conscious in a dream is enough to make most wake up, but with practice, it is possible to stay and experience a time and place that seems dream to you, yet is very real to those around you. Imagine it—whatever is done greatly impacts those inhabiting that reality. Controlling lucidity and moving through our multiverse is very powerful.

The energies we call gods use this power. They use dreamers to push realities in directions that create cultures that perpetuate their myths, even if that is based on fear. Scared people search for security, safety, protection, and deities provide just that, at least in story. It is enough for both human and god. Most helping the gods don't even remember what they have done. There are many that do, that live for sleep, that live to dream, so that they can please their god. Ancient peoples knew this. Their stories and sagas are filled with tales of gods interfering, meddling in the affairs of man, but they need hands to do so, and their devotees willingly offer theirs.

In realities that have no knowledge of Mariam of Okhum, then a devotee helped push your world in a direction towards patriarchy and war. She is unknown in those places because she was suffocated in her crib by the hands of a dreamer. In other realities a young president was shot, with the gunman captured insisting he was a patsy— because he was. The real person firing the fatal shot was never caught, because she was no longer in that reality. She woke up. In others a Macedon named Alexander became The Great, and ruled an empire that covered the known globe until he died an old, old man. Elsewhen, he died a young man, after conquering half a globe, poisoned while on campaign, or he was killed in his crib, or he was not even born when his mother, Olympias, met an untimely end. There are too many examples, from many, many realities.

There are also dreamers trying to stop the devoted ones. That's why the library at Alexandria never burned, how we enjoy Christopher Marlowe's plays, why the western hemisphere is Chinese … in some realities, anyway. Resisting the gods. Good luck with that, right? Those resistors are mostly just trying to protect what they call reality, which means being there to stop other dreamers.

They both tried to recruit me, but I prefer to work alone. I saw another type of dreamer, one that also works alone, and I think my energies are best spent there. I don't see I have much choice, because I don't see any others trying to stop them. But I don't stop a dreamer; I find them and I wait until they're awake. When they're awake, it is playing for real. That kind of death is not one they'll wake up from. I find them while they are feeling safe in their own reality, where a bartender thinks they're just another drunk, their colleagues think they're just another incompetent bureaucrat, and their mothers think they're a good son.

Sometimes it is a daughter. But not very often.

I climbed on a barstool one away from his and set my empty glass down. My eyes went to him, then shyly back to my glass. As if on cue, an ice cube shifted in the bottom.

I have a ritual of sorts before entering the dream state. I prepare my bed, propping pillows so that I recline more than lie. I turn off the lights and lie down, close my eyes and clear my mind by meditating on my breath. Just watching the air go in my nostrils, and then out, which settles my mind, tells it that its day of thinking is over, and that I need it to focus. Breath in, breath out. I then concentrate on the emptiness of no-thought, on the black behind the black you see when eyes are closed. As I sink deep into this blankness, I hold an intention. Intention is the key. Whether it is simply to remember a dream, or to go to a specific time or place, it is intention that directs the mind. With practice, an intention can be visualised as an image, or an icon, a manifestation of the meaning behind what is intended.

I held an image of my intention fiercely with concentration, the place she was killed, the darkness of night, a later night, when he would kill again. And I sank into the blackness, maintaining a thread of awareness as my body drifted into sleep. I just had to smell the air to hunt him. That scent of fear. Fear was his power. I breathed in the smell of his presence, and opened my eyes. I was in a dark lane, wearing the same skirt and smock as the other women, though no one, woman or man, was out at this time. Almost. I listened to the night and heard a soft noise, a distant breathing. I hoped it wasn't what I thought.

Gathering up the loose fabric of my dress, I crept forward, knowing I was already too late, at least for the young woman under him. His seventh victim. By the time I slipped around the corner, hiding in the shadows, her body lay on the cobblestones, legs splayed and blood flowing from her throat, soaking into the fabric of her bodice and the stones beneath. Ignoring her, I stepped past, and then I saw him. His back was turned as he faced the wall of a house. I knew his eyes were closed, and he was falling into a blackness of sorts, falling awake to his own reality. I watched him begin to grow translucent as he left this time and place, disappearing into the night. But before he vanished completely, I latched onto his image and followed, closing my eyes, falling forward, not onto the blood-stained cobbled lane but into his waking.

When I opened my eyes, I saw a brownstone building, beginning to wake for the new day. Fresh sunlight bathed the street. My only company at this time in the morning were the birds hidden in the trees above. They were the only things singing in this place. I marked the scene firmly in my mind, the look, the feel, the smell. It would be the intention I would use to return to this waking, when I would wait for him to leave the safety of his apartment, his bed, and emerge outside in the reality where he felt safe. I would follow him down the seedy street to his favourite seedy bar, where I could sit next to him and he could buy me a drink.

"I'm empty," I said with a shrug. That I have to wait at all says so much about the guy. Finally, he lifted a finger to the bartender and mumbled something like, "two of those."

"Doubles," I added, smiling. I flash it at my target, a nice shiny lure, followed by a jokey tug at the line. I seem to like fishing analogies today. "Their bourbon is so weak!"

He smirked in reply.

I softened my face, trying for inviting, safe, horny. I could see I pulled it off. He relaxed, as if that inner battle with his rational mind ended and I won. He's not used to this. Women don't approach him, even in a place like here. I caught a glimpse of the frightened little boy lurking deep inside him, but I pushed that image away. I'm not here to save children. I am here for the man who rapes and kills young women.

When the glasses arrived, I indicated to the stool next to his and he nodded. I moved closer.

"I need this after the day I've had," I told him. "Thanks."

"My pleasure," he responded.

I make up a story about a shitty boss, a frustrating job, and he nods. He can relate to that. I tell him that even with the sun shining outside I sometimes want to just hide from this city. It's no Ritz, he admits, but this place is good to sometimes slink away to. I watch as he sips his drink after I do mine. It's his third and he is loosening up, deciding he likes me and flattered that I seem to like him. Women don't talk to him like this and he likes it. What man wouldn't? The chat continues to float along the surface. I slip in a flirt, a subtle innuendo. It takes him a few moments to realise that that is what it is. He smiles. His guard is down. I turn my head to listen to the music from a jukebox in the corner. The music in this decade is spectacularly terrible.

"Shall we dance?" I ask.

He smiles and nods. I take his hand and am pleased it is already open and waiting. We take a few steps away from the bar and I put my arm around him, placing my palm against the small of his back and slowly move it up. I put the other around his waist and place myself so smoothly against him that he thinks he put me there. I want him to feel my breasts against his chest, my warm body next to his. I feel his hands around my back. One tentatively moves lower. After a few more sways to the music, I encourage it to keep traveling, and it cups my ass. I feel a bulge against my thigh.

We sway some more. His hand is still on my ass. The bulge presses against my leg. I nuzzle my face into his neck. He smells my hair. I know his eyes are closed and he has made a decision. He will take me home.

"I'd rather dance someplace more private," I whisper as the next song starts.

I'll decide what I do on the walk over, or maybe as events unfold. Let him go in first, exposing his back? Surprise him when he starts to undress, pants around his ankles? Wait until he is on top of me, totally lost in the moment, totally vulnerable?

Either way, the result will be the same.

Failure to Communicate

We can't even communicate with dolphins, an intelligent mammal from our own planet. What on earth (or off it) makes us think we could talk to alien life when they finally show up?

The ship arrived on a Tuesday. Everybody would remember where they were, and what they were doing, the moment they looked up and saw it. First contact. We were no longer alone. It sat in a low orbit, silently circling our blue green planet. Its size made it visible to the naked eye, day and night. It seemed to come from nowhere, totally undetected, and it circled.

Silently.

Hours turned into days, days into weeks, fear and excitement warped into fear and confusion. We all waited, watching as the huge silver disk slid over our homes. The welcome signs of the new-agers began to fade. The dooms-dayers grew bored in their bunkers. Militaries scrambled and then grew restless. The International Space Station readied to evacuate, then just watched and waited.

Every effort to communicate failed. As the days went by the world collectively began to exhale after realising it was holding its breath, expecting something to happen.

And nothing was happening. Finally, as a month came to an end, it left as silently as it arrived.

Easton raised her hand to silence the room. It wasn't necessary. They'd all come to hear her announcement. They all knew what it would be. She sat at her usual place at the head of the oblong wooden table. Her heads of department and essential brain power filled the seats surrounding it. Others stood along the walls and at the back of the meeting room.

"I want to say right now," she began, "this is going to be totally voluntary. Taking any part in what we do from this point on will be a federal offence. The government has banned any private attempts to reach our visitors." She looked at the assembled team, trying to make eye contact with each person. "But I think we've all had enough of them sitting on their hands."

They continued to watch her, waiting for the words.

"I'd like to go and meet our guests," she said. Murmurs and nods rippled around the room. "I want to take her up." She scanned the team again. "I need to say this again. Participation is voluntary. If you don't feel comfortable with what I am asking you to do, you are excused, no ramifications on your employment. See it as a paid vacation, and come back when the dust settles, knowing you are still a valued member of the team."

She waited. Nobody moved from their chairs. Nobody moved towards the door.

"Objections?" she asked.

"She's still in trials," Anderton said.

"I appreciate that," Easton replied. "I appreciate you pointing it out. I want to see all hats being worn here, not just the gung-ho colour."

"So …" Anderton started.

"So, we've had two trials," Easton said. "Two successful trials."

"… out of a scheduled five. Going orbital is still too new to risk life and ship."

"I hear you, Anderton." She turned towards a man sitting to his left. "Hadley, it's your department. Is she fit enough? Can she do it?"

"She can do it," Hadley replied.

"How long until she can be ready for launch?" she asked.

"Two days. Fuelling and safety checks," her ground team manager said. "We were already prepping for the third trial."

"So, you're saying one day, working a twenty four hour shift?" Easton asked.

"Doable," Hadley said after a pause.

"I'm hearing my voice a lot at the moment. I know that's nothing new," Easton said. "I need to hear from you."

"They'll try to stop us." Langdon, flight control.

"We'll do it in secret, come out of the hanger at the last minute …" Coombs, mission control.

"They're already watching all the private spaceports. They'll notice the activity." Ogden, engineering.

They were a good team, picked for moments like these, mused Easton. "Paretti?" she asked.

"One step ahead of you," Paretti said. "We'll have a little emergency out back and spend all night clearing it up. Something to keep us busy all night. Or at least look that way. Maybe a small explosion and fire."

"I thought there was a reason for that grin on your face." Laughter eased the tension in the room. A little, at least.

"And I'm sorry, Sims," she said, turning to a trim figure midway around the table. "It's going to be me. I can't ask this of anyone."

"I've trained for this, ma'am. I'm your pilot," Sims said.

"And now you'll finish my training. We have a little over twenty four hours."

"Ma'am!" protested Sims. He clenched his fists under the table and worked his jaw muscles. The retired military officer rarely raised his voice to a superior and had never questioned their orders while an audience was present, a habit and discipline he carried into civilian life.

"I'm sorry, Sims. I truly am. But this is why I built our bird, that's why I've been shadowing you, and that's how it's going to go. I've been dreaming of this my entire life."

"Yes, Ma'am," Sims answered formally.

Easton inhaled deeply and slowly exhaled. "Right, then," she said. "Any more questions?"

All present answered with a tangible eagerness. "You all know what you're doing. It's time to do it. Get your teams moving. Let's go meet our guests."

Chairs were pushed back as the team members dispersed.

Easton strapped into the pilot seat. She moved to rub her tired eyes and her gloved hand hit the faceplate of her helmet. She shook her head, hoping the stimulant would kick in soon. Sims guided her through the extensive safety checks. The test pilot was formal and efficient in the hours spent with his boss during the night, relaxing with acceptance of his newer role of mentor. *His* trip would be in his bosses' ear, a private line with visual feed and remote override should he need it. It was actually safer this way, he grudgingly admitted.

Easton looked to her left and nodded to *Motherbird's* primary pilot. Turning right she acknowledged *Motherbird's* second pilot.

"*Magpie* ready for flight," she reported.

"Acknowledged, *Magpie. Motherbird* ready for flight," the primary pilot said, dispensing with the codes and phrases used during the night in case other listeners were tuning in as usual.

The trucks tasked with towing *Motherbird* started their engines. Easton blinked in the morning light as the hangar doors began to slide open. She ran her gaze over the length of the massive wing, half a football field in length. She felt small but safe nestled in the middle, a little fledgling chick held in the wings of its protective parent. The trucks pulled the crafts into the bright morning sun and onto the desert runway.

"Just got a call from the Air Force, ma'am," Coombs said over the radio.

"We're only cleaning out the hangar," Easton said.

"That's what I told them."

The trucks detached from *Motherbird*. The pilots started the engines and carried out their own pre-flight checks. The big plane and its little spaceship trundled towards the long, wide stretch of tarmac for their take off.

"*Motherbird*, clear for take-off," air traffic control said.

"We have just been issued a warning to desist," Coombs said.

"Ignore them," Easton replied.

Motherbird increased speed until the runway became a blur. As the dry hills in the distance grew closer Easton felt the force of take-off push her into the seat, and the hills disappeared underneath. *Motherbird* continued to accelerate as she banked in her climb, an upward spiral taking them to the plane's service ceiling of twenty-five thousand meters. She watched *Motherbird's* pilots as they worked with a cold professionalism.

"Airforce is scrambling jets to intercept. They say they will shoot you down," Coombs said.

"Ignore them," Easton answered. "They wouldn't dare." She saw the primary pilot laugh under his breathing mask. Professional, but not cold, she amended. "Turn off the radio if you prefer."

"Thirty minutes to release ma'am," Sims said in her ear. "Scan the readings for me, and conduct your preparations."

Easton moved her helmet over the dials so Sims could use the camera mounted on it and read them all, confirming what he saw on his own controls in the control room below. She worked through the pre-release check list, item by tedious item.

A fighter jet joined their sky, stationing itself off the right wing. Another positioned itself off the left. From her position in the middle Easton couldn't see, but was sure the fighter pilots were motioning for *Motherbird* to descend, thumb pointing downward, hand moving down. That's what they did in the movies, anyway. The silence told her *Motherbird's* pilots had turned the radio off.

And the pressure of her body against the seat told her they were still climbing. The fighters re-positioned themselves in front of *Motherbird*. They continued to climb. As they approached the fighter's ceiling limit both pulled away from the large plane. Easton craned her neck to watch them fade to small dots in the distance.

"Told you," Easton said to Sims. "We're doing what they wished they could. Open all channels and let everybody listen now. This isn't just for us."

"Focus on your task, ma'am," Sims said. "Reaching release point. You know what to do. On my command."

Both Easton and Sim's hands hovered over the release switch, one just beneath the thermosphere, the other in a desert space port.

"Good luck, ma'am," Sims added. "And three … two … one … Release! Release! Release!"

Easton pulled the switch. She felt herself float upwards, held in place by the safety straps, as *Magpie* detached and fell away. *Motherbird* turned sharply for her long descent and at the same time Easton slammed back into the chair as *Magpie's* rocket ignited. Her head snapped back in her helmet. The small craft rattled and shuddered. Her vision blurred as the force of acceleration squeezed the air out of her lungs. And then, just when she thought she would pass out, it stopped. The sound. The pressure. The sky darkened until it became black, and Easton was in space. She stared at the vast expanse, mouth open and mind dazed.

"Report, ma'am," Sims commanded.

"Adjusting course now," Easton said, using the thrusters. The stars tilted until they were lost to view, eclipsed by the glowing silver sphere of the visiting spaceship in front of her.

"Watch your roll, ma'am. Correct yaw zero one three degrees. Fire reverse thrusters to reduce speed."

Easton worked the controls. The Visitors' ship began to slowly drift out of view.

"You're over correcting, ma'am," Sims said.

Easton manipulated the thrusters again. The huge silver ship slipped away faster.

"Take your hands away from the controls, ma'am. I am overriding," Sims said.

Easton opened her hands and slowly took them away from the control panel. She rested them on her knees and watched the Visitors' ship return to centre view. It encompassed her entire vision.

"You like to talk, ma'am," Sims said. "The world is listening. Tell them what you see."

"I ..." Easton began. "It's enormous. And beautiful. It appears to have a smooth surface, entirely smooth, everywhere I look. No windows, just ... no, not smooth ... a glow, a silvery glow ... I ...."

"It's Ok, ma'am. Video link is functioning perfectly. We can all see what you are seeing ..."

Easton sat in the small cockpit as Sims brought the craft closer. The seconds ticked by. She tried her radio to contact the alien craft, but, just as she expected, there was no response.

"Take me closer," she told Sims.

She felt a soft nudge to her back as he complied and the ship filled more and more of the view until all she could see was the glow of the sphere in front of her. She continued forward and the glow seemed to invade the cockpit like condensation on glass. She rubbed her view plate with a gloved hand but a haze remained.

"Sims, that's close enough for now," she said.

"Sims!" she shouted when there was no response.

Only silence answered her. *Magpie* continued to drift forward as the glow of the Visitors' ship increased around her. Easton felt a panic begin deep down in her gut, a fear that started to drag itself upward, clawing its way out. Her focus and self-discipline clamped down on it like a steel fist, stopping it from rising, at least for the moment. She gripped the controls and slowed *Magpie* with bow thrusters. Words formed, a call to Sims, a plea for help, a demand for action, but she heard nothing, each syllable and letter dissolving as it left her mouth.

She stared at her hands in the growing glow, trying to focus, trying to will them to act on the controls, to feel their touch, but each finger seemed to disappear as she watched, followed by her hands and her wrists. The glow filled the cockpit until all Easton could see was white. She closed her eyes and the glow filled the space in the dark of her mind. She didn't know if her eyes were open or closed, if her hands held controls, if she sat in her chair, or if … Easton felt the glow consume her. She felt herself dissolving into the light. A flicker of a thought held onto who or what she was, a memory both intimate and distant. It was the only grip she had on who or what existed before this present moment. Her tenuous hold threatened to slip into the same void Easton felt herself becoming. She was at the same time everything that filled the vastness of the universe as well as the smallest of elementary particles.

Easton felt herself let go of everything she knew, of concepts, of image, of language and word, of herself. She felt filled with a … love … a joy … something beyond words inviting wholeness through dissolution. She wanted to accept the invitation, but a sliver of consciousness held her back. The glow caressed her mind, holding all thought, gently pulling it into the sphere. The small splinter of her identity sensed the others, somehow knowing that there was no place for fear, that, in some way beyond comprehension, beckoned her to let go. But she had no ears to hear, no hands to feel, nose to smell, tongue to taste, mind to think … the only tools she had to interpret her reality were gone. She hung, suspended, between mystery and knowing, between experience and confusion, on the other side of a door she did not know how to open.

Then something encroached, forming a concept that demanded attention. She tried to ignore it, to stay in this place, this state, but the concept pulled too hard and she turned her attention to it.

It was a colour. Something deep within told her that the colour had a meaning. Her mind tried to puzzle this new message.

A red light flashed on the control panel and the ship's computer cut in. "Oxygen levels nearing critical," the program announced.

The red light continued to flash. The computer repeated its warning. Easton felt a gentle hand on her sternum pushing down as the bow thrusters fired. Her vision cleared and she saw that it was her own hands on the controls that caused it.

"*Magpie*, this is flight control! Do you read?" the speaker in her helmet said.

"*Magpie*, please respond!" it demanded.

"Sarah, are you there?"

Words and concepts filled her mind. Sound—a physical wave that carried ideas. Sarah Easton breathed in slowly, experiencing the sensation of air entering her body, filling her lungs, expanding her chest. She exhaled, and the warmer air tickle her upper lip—a physical, tangible act. Her clearing mind told her that words were needed, to manifest thought in a physical form. She moved her mouth, awkwardly trying to form them.

"I'm here," she managed to say.

"Thank God for that!" Sims said. "We lost contact with you. You just disappeared. What happened?" he asked.

She sat gazing at the glowing orb orbiting above the earth. To her eyes, it looked, once again, like the ship that appeared in the sky so many weeks before. She tried to feel it, to *sense* it, as a part of her seemed to vaguely remember, but memory slipped away like dreams in the morning.

She searched for words to describe what seemed beyond concept, what was beyond words.

"I don't know," she said after a moment, giving up.

Magpie slowly turned under Sim's control and began its long glide home.

The Visitors approached the glowing orb with wonder and reverence. They neared the pulsing light and slowed, stopping as close as was wise. They opened their minds and their hearts and were embraced. They touched the colours that danced and swirled around the planet. Or rather, they let the colours touch them. They swirled and danced, losing themselves in the beautiful vibrating energy, sharing in the wholeness.

So rarely had they encountered such a celebration of life, a planet breathing existence in such a myriad of forms! Each form with its own unique signature, its own wavelength, its own colours, yet all inseparable, united with the one magnificent organism that the Visitors had come all this way to honour. The Visitors shared their existence. They offered their blessings. And they received blessings. The blue-green planet touched them, and thanked them.

In their timeless way, the Visitors would always be sharing, always be blessed, just as the magnificent life filled orb, circling its star in this corner of the galaxy, would always be sharing and blessing.

When the lifeless grey moon completed one circle of its beautiful host, they left, continuing their endless pilgrimage in search of other orbs of life, to commune and celebrate and worship.

Stepping Out: The Personal Log of Captain Elizabeth Sheridan

In a future where faster than light travel is possible, we scour the galaxy for a Planet B, only to find there is none. The despondent crew of the Fortitude take the decision to give up the search and return to their ailing home planet, Earth.

Introduction

After the exploratory ship *Fortitude* returned to Earth, everything changed. The crew of the *Fortitude* had already taken multiple Steps prior to the discovery of planet Kepler 76-e, now known as Shackleton, or more popularly as 'The Shack.' It was so named to reflect our own collective "Shackleton Moment," when the people of Earth wisely decided to turn back, to admit that the prize, while worthy, was out of our reach, and the only way to save humanity was to focus on our planet.

In 1908, Ernest Shackleton's prize was the South Pole. It was a time of exploration, filled with toughened heroes, the celebrities of their day. He could have continued and been remembered as the first man to reach the pole. But he would have died on the return, just as his contemporary, Robert Scott, did a few years later.

Shackleton turned back, and in doing so, he saved his men. Similarly, we turned back, and in doing so, we saved ourselves. The crew of the *Fortitude* was in the depths of space for over sixteen years. Captain Elizabeth Sheridan had no way of knowing that the story of the *Fortitude*, of the disappointment the crew experienced, and the crushing despondency they felt when they decided to turn back, would have impacted humanity the way it did.

Kepler 76-e is the fifth planet orbiting a Sol-like star, located 2089 light-years from Earth. It is situated in the Goldilocks Zone, the habitable area around a star where the temperature is just right— not too hot and not too cold—for water to exist on a planet in liquid form. However, it wasn't merely water that the *Fortitude*, and many other exploratory ships, sought.

They were looking for life. Every planet so far discovered, and this is true to the present day, is devoid of life, even in fossilised form. Many of these planets contain water, both liquid and frozen, but none hold even the most primitive type of life. On our Earth, life first began over 3.5 billion years ago, maybe even over 4 billion years in the past. Not long after our oceans formed, microscopic single-celled organisms emerged, then grew and evolved into the myriad forms of life we celebrate today.

Early theories held that life on Earth might have come from biological matter carried by space dust or meteorites. We no longer believe this to be viable hypothesis. Earth is unique among trillions of planets orbiting billions of stars. Our Milky Way Galaxy, comprising over 200 billion stars, is itself one of perhaps two billion galaxies in the known universe.

And yet, as far as we can find, life is only known on planet Earth. Our home.

While Captain Sheridan and her crew Stepped back to Earth, despairing in what they perceived as their failure, today we see their discovery and voyage differently. Captain Sheridan, in her own words, "gave up." And when the *Fortitude* and its sole surviving crew member returned to Earth, we all, also, gave up. But in giving up, in losing hope that there was a new start or a sanctuary somewhere in the stars, we began to value what we had.

We will still reach out to the stars. We will still study and settle the planets we find, building new homes from bare rock, and mining their rich resources. We will still search for life. But not like before. Through her grief, Captain Sheridan helped us see that we need to value what we have. The planets that have been, and are still being discovered, can never provide enough to meet humanity's need for air to breath, land to farm, or oceans to fish. As news of the fate of the *Fortitude* spread around the globe, and especially after the publication of her personal log, Elizabeth Sheridan shocked a generation into action, initiating what would be known as *The Great Clean-Up*. During its time, it was called other things, with similar themes: the seventh generation, the waking up, a coming to our senses, taking responsibility, planning for a future. It was a true turning point— a pivotal decision.

I am honored to write the introduction to this reprint of Captain Sheridan's brief log, a record she began to keep only after she and her crew realised that the beautiful green of The Shack one sees from space was only rock. Although she may not have known it at the time, what she penned was a wake-up call. I like to think that she knew, somewhere deep down, that that was what her words would become. She was the leader of the expedition, but also served as ship's doctor. Her deep concern for her crew fills her journal, but so too does her concern for those left behind on Earth. It is nice to believe, if perhaps only a sentimental notion, that that was what motivated her to write them. If you are fortunate to view the original copy of her log kept at the United Nations Museum at Geneva, Switzerland, you will see that she did not date her entries. She seemed to let the pain inside her escape onto the page nearest to her pen at the time. This reproduction of her personal log has tried to stay true to how she wrote it. Footnotes have been added as an editorial device to help with the understanding of some terminology and references used. These have been placed at the end of the text so that continuity is not disrupted.

Astrogator and astrophysicist Alan Seed was the only crew member of the *Fortitude* to return to Earth. As promised to Captain Sheridan, he shared the story of their exploration as well as her personal log. Their experience was not solitary. In the years immediately after the return of the *Fortitude*, other ships returned with core samples from barren rocky planets. None found the hoped-for sister to our home. Their failure mirrored that of the *Fortitude*, and personal accounts of their crew reflected the despondency felt by Sheridan and her crew. As more ships returned home, their logs were similarly published. But none had the effect of the first by the captain of the *Fortitude*. The return of the others gave it even more power.

We all owe her, and her crew, a great deal of gratitude. While Elizabeth Sheridan, and many of those with her, chose to 'step out' 2000 light-years from home, they will always be with us.

Jimena Ruiz, Secretary General of the United Nations

Geneva, Switzerland

The Personal Log of Captain Elizabeth Sheridan

I instructed the crew to cease geological surveys of the surface of Kepler 76-e. Nate refused. I have to find an opportunity to apologise to him. When I ordered the ground crew up, he said, "No. It's too soon."

I made myself listen to the recording. Then I deleted it from the record.

"It's not too soon," I told him. "It's already too late. It's time to go home."

For me, it is. I didn't quite know it on the bridge speaking to the survey crew at that moment, at least not consciously. But the decision brought relief.

Not to Nate. "No," he said. I could hear his anger; he didn't mask it. "What are you doing, *ordering* me?"

"Yes, Nate," I said. "Return to the ship so we can prep for return to the Ein-Ros." (1)

"No!" he said.

"This is an order, Mr. Huckins! Return to the ship."

"No. What are you going to do about it?"

We reduced ourselves to bickering children. The Captain and First Mate of an interstellar ship throwing tantrums. In hindsight, it's easy to remember that arguing with a child is a no-win situation. The child always wins. When there's no adult involved, it can only go badly.

"Refusing an order is mutiny!" I actually said that.

"Fuck you, Liz. This isn't the military."

I did the only thing I could. I shut up. Dead air filled the comms between us. Finally, I said, "Be careful down there." (2)

I waited for a reply, but none came. They would be back in two cycles; that's all they had supplies for. Forty-eight hours to clean up my mess. From his chair at navigation, Alan stared blankly at me, probably too confused or shocked to register what he just witnessed. At the time I wanted him to intervene, to take over, deem me unfit to continue command. I pleaded with my eyes, but he couldn't or wouldn't translate. Nobody wants to be in my shoes. I don't want to be in my shoes.

*

The survey party returned today. I went to Nate's cabin and stood in front of the door for several minutes, wanting to walk away, wanting to pretend what happened didn't. But I didn't have that kind of out. His door slid open when I knocked. He was standing in the middle of his cabin. I walked towards him, put my arms around him and he started to sob. Our tears soaked the backs of each other's necks. I don't remember going to his bunk, but that is where we stayed, holding each other, crying.

*

The ship is quiet. Like a coffin. I gave instructions to Alan to plot the most efficient Steps home. It's likely all the crew feels the same way, but it is ultimately my decision. The responsibility is all mine. I am reassured by the lack of opposition. I expected more of a fight. At least an argument. Shouting. Storming out. But they just stared at me, resigned. They are tired of searching for something that none of us believe we will ever find. Nate almost looked sympathetic. They can all blame me.

Alan didn't look up from his work. He leaned over his screen, exploring trajectories, calculating fuel ratios, adjusting computations. Gary secluded himself in 'his' reactor room, prepping for acceleration. I tried to busy myself in the sickbay, tidying already orderly supplies. There's not much I could do. I've been too neat of a ship's doctor. I was tempted to reorder all medicines alphabetically—demerol, dextroamphetamine, diazepam, nitrazepam, temazepam, xylocaine. I put quite a few in their own cabinet and locked it. How will I hide the key from myself? We move numbly. I fear when I can feel again, knowing where the key is. The cannabinoids are now in a glass-doored cabinet that used to house bandages, those with higher THC content to the front so they can be easily seen. Hopefully some will help themselves to this 'first aid.' I lack the ability to help myself. That is a sure sign of depression—having a helpful medicine at hand but not being able to bring myself to use it.

*

I sat on the bridge staring at the planet for hours. The green is the first I have seen, that any of us have seen since we … left. Why is that such a hard word to write? World after world of barren rock and poison air, of excitement and anticipation giving over to disappointment after disappointment.

Green. Fields of green, wrapping this lonely place. Dark and rich. Swathes of velvet. White clouds swirled in the atmosphere, winds dragging long tails over dark continents. A large spiralling storm formed a brooch on her green gown. If I didn't know how dead it was, I would have thought it so beautiful from here. Maybe it is, but I've seen far too many dead worlds to find beauty in any of them.

When I was a girl, there was a small field outside of town. I made the mistake of returning before leaving, visiting my old home, somehow knowing I would never return. It was gone. Built over. Dead. Dying, like the planet itself. It made me secure in my decision to leave Earth on the *Fortitude*. I would find a new home for all of us, a green place, a healthy place. Our first Step was so exciting. The anticipation, the exhilaration. Eight months building up to discovering nothing but a wind-blown rock. But we carried on. Another year sheltering from solar radiation behind an inner planet or moon while the Ein-Ros faced the star, absorbing and converting photons into the incredible amounts of energy needed. Then a Step, and another discovery. Deeper into the unknown. Another Step, farther than anybody had ever Stepped, and were rewarded with water! (3) Dark rivers emerging from underground, flowing into vast alluvial plains and disappearing into fine sands, returning to its subterranean sea. Kristin spent weeks analysing it at the molecular level. But the results were the same. Devoid of any life. So, we kept going.

Green. Green. Green. Green. Green. (4)

I tried to remember what that field smelled like when I was a girl. I must have been sitting, eyes on the screen, for several hours. Alan startled me back to the moment, saying my name. He held out a mug of coffee and a handful of tissues. My cheeks were wet. Snot ran down my chin. I took the tissues and wiped my face. I tried to meet his eyes as I took the drink, but he was looking down. I think he was crying too.

*

Acceleration has increased gravity on the ship to 1.4. It mirrors our mood. The Ein-Ros is three months away. I am so heavy. Weighed down. A leaden hand pushing from the center of my heart, down, down, down. I fear all crew feels the same. It will be at least two weeks until we reach peak velocity and power down the reactor. So. Heavy.

*

The watch system has started to break down. I couldn't sleep, again, so I went to the bridge. Nate was alone. Kristin has not come out of her cabin for several cycles. Our dear astrobiologist. Her primary role was to study new life. She wanted to be the first to see it and study it. First contact, even if through a microscope. Every Step brought a new level of frustration and disappointment. To Kristin, astrobiology wasn't just about an evolutionary record, but the future of life in the universe. The future of our life in the universe. But all she found was … not death … but the lack of life. The impossibility of life. She tested algae and moss in the atmospheres, samples of the hardiest high-altitude plants from Earth. None survived. She developed an obsession with the rocks, grinding them ever smaller, insisting there was something 'between the molecules.' She'll have lots of time on the trip back to study it. If Dana gives her access to her core samples.

Gary is with the reactor all the time. There's none of his usual humour at the mess table. I don't even know if he's eating. I had to order him to let me in. He looks like he hasn't slept since … I don't know. He spoke in single words, and only in answer to questions. I gave him a sedative, a sleeping pill. He held it in his hand, looking confused. He caught me glancing at the reactor with a look of worry I didn't have the strength to hide.

"She'll be ok," he said. A hoarse whisper, an actual complete sentence. If he'd listen, I would confine him to sick bay. I'd confine all of us, force sedatives and sleep. But the chain of command seems to have broken down as well.

*

Kristin didn't answer my knocks at her cabin door. I overrode the lock, and when the door slid open, it was empty. Her bed was unmade. The room smelled of an unwashed body. Her papers had been strewn over the floor. Her notebooks toppled from a shelf as if they were thrown. Cynthia lay in the corner among broken glass and spilled soil. Each leaf of her *aspidistra elatior (5)* was sprinkled around her quarters, torn into smaller and smaller pieces. I searched the mess hall, the sickbay, the washroom, but could not find her. I called over ship's comms but got no response. I demanded the bridge answer. Dana eventually reported she was alone there. That she had not seen Kristin. Each answer had to be pulled out of her. I need to go to the reactor room. Gary will not reply.

*

The starboard outer airlock door was open. I wouldn't have noticed if I hadn't stopped to look into the only place I had not yet checked. The airlock is manually controlled from the inside and only operates if the inner door is sealed. From the inside. It could only have been done deliberately, by somebody determined to get out. The alarm would have to have been disengaged, which it was.

I checked all the suits. One should be missing, but they are all there, hanging by each of our lockers.

Please, Kristin. Prove me wrong.

*

I assembled all crew in the mess. Kristin's seat was empty.

"Kristin has stepped out," I said. The conversation burned into my memory.

It was something we all knew, but the words had to be spoken aloud. To make it real. We sat as silently as tears ran down our cheeks.

"Like Oates (6)," Dana said. Softly. But we all heard.

"No, Dana," I said. "Not like that. Not like that at all. We all feel bad. But stepping out is not saving anybody. Kristin wasn't holding us back. None of you are holding us back. We're not struggling to survive on some godforsaken icefield. We're just trying to get home. We're stronger together." I tried to sound like what I said held truth, but part of me envied Kristin.

The crew stared blankly at me. "Nobody is to be alone until I say. We need to rely on each other until we get through this. We can't be trusted by ourselves."

I was encouraged by the lack of resistance. "Nate and Gary will bunk and work together. Dana, you will partner with Alan."

"Clear?" I asked loudly, summoning an illusion of authority.

"Clear." Murmurs around the table.

"What about you?" Alan asked.

"I'll rely on all of you," I lied. "We'll remember Kristin when we flip for deceleration (7)."

After leaving the mess, I returned to the airlock. *Oh, Kristin.* I closed the outer door and secured the exit.

*

Flip and Decel. Preparations have kept us busy. Moving mass, inspecting the reactor. I assigned both teams to go over it, more to double-check Gary's work. The room is usually spotless, but there are worrying signs. Discarded food packets covered the floor. Glass panels were smudged with dirty fingers. Spilled mass. I had to leave the room before I lost control. Spilled mass! Infused deuterium pellets just lying about the deck! I felt so angry. Alan helped me go out, almost pushed me, and closed the door behind me.

Anger is a symptom of frustration. Frustration is a product of stress, of a lack of understanding. I remember the seminars before leaving. Psychologists speculating on what we might feel after years in space. They had no idea. *Use and develop the tools you can to show patience, acceptance, and trust.* Lucky for them now that they are so far away from me. So far away.

*

The star grows larger in the viewscreen. We'll be docking with the Ein-Ros and leaving this system soon. Not soon enough. Once docking is complete Alan will go alone to initiate Step. He won't allow any other crew to join him in that inner sanctum. He never has.

*

I have to trust Alan in the control room, at the centre of the Ein-Ros, monitoring the quantum computer that is calculating our Step, his only company an AI that speaks in coordinates. Alan has been very withdrawn but speaks with me when I ask. Nate and Gary talk to each other quietly. It's not my imagination that they go silent whenever I am around, or when they notice I am near. I have nobody to talk to.

*

Step. I usually dread the manoeuvre, the way it seems to stretch my body in all directions at the same time. Regardless, there used to be some anticipation, an excitement. Going farther than anyone has ever gone before. This time we're just trying to go back. Pointless pain. I don't even know what home is anymore. This ship has been my home. The crew, my family. Now the ship is only … a means to an end? An end none of us wanted? And my crew are like strangers. I don't even know myself anymore.

After the Step, Alan returned to the *Fortitude*. There was no celebration. No traditional drinks. No welcome back. No thanks. We only went backwards for the first time. We will wait behind an inner planet while the Ein-Ros recharges. Alan estimates it will take five months to collect enough power for the next step. He plotted a four Step route back to Earth, utilizing maximum power to increase the distance of each Step. He has identified several larger G class stars with recorded exoplanets to shelter behind while the Ein-Ros builds up the power it needs. There is a risk the quantum computer can become damaged with the extra demands. But if it means a quicker way back, we all find the risk acceptable.

*

Freefall is making me weak. Floating like a ghost. It doesn't matter. I keep losing track of hours and cycles. We must be nearing time to re-join the Ein-Ros and Step. What will we tell them? That we failed? That nothing is out there? "Sorry guys, we couldn't save you. We're all going to die." I don't want to face that.

*

Nate and Gary are gone. They stepped out together. They hacked the starboard air lock. Gary left a note on the wall of the reactor room, but we can't make any sense of it. Gary probably couldn't either. Lines slanting down the page. The reactor room is a mess. Squiggles of shit smear the walls. Globules of piss float in the air. Both he and Nate must have holed up in there, not even leaving to relieve themselves. I know I should feel more, I should cry or … anything. But I can't. And to be honest, I am glad I don't.

Dana is still talking to herself. She rolls her eyes and lapses into silence, but then snaps out of it and goes back to her conversation. Long babbling monologues that make no sense. Coaxing her to sick bay I tried to give her a sedative, but she swung her arm and hit me away. I floated to the bulkhead and hit my back on a cabinet. By the time I steadied myself, she was out the door.

*

Alan found Dana drifting in the loading bay, near her core samples.

We used the port airlock to dispose of her body.

*

I had the dream again; at least I think it is a dream. I may not have been asleep. I am not always certain when I am. I was barefoot, walking on green grass. Each cold damp blade tickled the soles of my feet. They were young feet. Or I was young. Yes, I think I am young, a girl, back on Earth, back at home, in the field we used to visit. The sky is the palest blue. It is so beautiful. I breathe the warm, unfiltered air. I walk on. But the grass is becoming rougher. My feet are covered in dust, and the grass is coarse and dry. The sky has lightened, a burnt dirtied blue. I walk on until I come to a stream. There should be water. I know that it once was water. Only now it is a dark sludge. The smell is overpowering. But I walk closer, to the bank and step into the stream. My feet sink into gooey mud, but the mud burns. I step in deeper. The water reaches my knees, and then my thighs. My skin is in agony, burning, blistering, being eaten away. I go deeper still until I am chest deep, then neck deep. It is agony. I exhale slowly and then sink under the surface. (8)

I write this down in the hope it will stop. I can still feel the burning.

*

The ship is on autopilot. It will dock with the Ein-Ros and then Step. Once in the solar system, it will detach, and accelerate towards Earth. Flip and Decel are programmed. Alan has promised to stay with the ship, to tell them what is out there, tell them to care (9). He said he will do that for me. We sat together in the bridge, his hand resting on mine. We spoke with our eyes. I heard what he was feeling, and I am certain he heard me. That he understands why I am giving up. His smile was so soft, so gentle. He has been a rock. You know what I mean, Alan.

I am not as ... brave as the rest of my crew. I am going to go to the medicine cabinet in sick bay and numb myself first. (10)

Footnotes

(1) At the time of Captain Sheridan, Donuts were referred to as Ein-Ros, in reference to the Einstein-Rosen bridge the devices created. (Editor)

(2) The official log for this date consists of one line: *Survey party continuing work planetside.* There is no recorded evidence of this interaction. (Editor)

(3) The planet Captain Sheridan is referring to is HAT-P-5b, the colony planet known colloquially as 'Hat Pin'. Its rivers of clear water, underground caverns and resource rich minerals has enabled it to grow into a significant center of mining and settlement. (Editor)

(4) This page in Captain Sheridan's original log is bordered in what looks like green pen. (Editor)

(5) *Aspidistra elatior* is the Cast-Iron plant. Astrobiologist and Hydrologist, Kristin Vaughn brought her plant, which she named Cynthia, with her from Earth. She nursed it for the sixteen years she was on the *Fortitude*. (Editor)

(6) Lawrence Edward Grace Oates accompanied Robert Falcon Scott on his ill-fated expedition to reach the South Pole. Afflicted with gangrene and frostbite, Captain Oates chose to die rather than be a burden to his companions, and thereby increase their chances of survival. He left his tent to freeze on the ice, saying as he went, "I am just going

outside and may be some time." The story of the *Terra Nova* Expedition was among many of the books in the library of the *Fortitude*, and crew were quite familiar with their contents. (Editor)

(7) There is no record in the official log of a ceremony being held for Kristin Vaughn, nor any other member of the crew. Just as Captain Sheridan's personal log became sporadic, with long periods of time elapsing between entries, the official ship's log similarly contained long periods with no entries. Only in the last three months of the return to Earth did astrogator and astrophysicist (and last remaining member of the crew of the *Fortitude*), Alan Seed, regularly record entries into the ship's log. (Editor)

(8) Some have tried to find the field that Captain Sheridan describes from her childhood. They maintain that the dreams that plagued her were not from her own subconscious, but visionary glimpses of what would meet her upon return to Earth. The town where she grew up did have several parcels of open land around it before urban sprawl consumed them. The exact location of her childhood 'park' is unknown. A commemorative plaque has been placed near the location of the house where she grew up. The stream she describes was no different from most waterways in and around urban centres at the time. Whether a reflection of subconscious fear, or mystical glimpse into what awaited, it is commonly accepted that the recurring nightmares Captain Sheridan experienced during her last weeks on the

Fortitude were a significant factor in her decision to step out. (Editor)

(9) Astrogator and astrophysicist Alan Seed honoured his promise to Captain Sheridan. He cooperated with the official investigation into the deaths of his crewmates, including handing over all confidential papers, such as the personal log of Elizabeth Sheridan. Three months after his return to Earth he stepped out, in his own fashion, and joined his captain and crewmates. (Editor)

(10) This is the last entry in Captain Elizabeth Sheridan's personal log. (Editor)

Maritime Report

During the harvesting of plastics in the Pacific Ocean as part of The Great Clean-Up, a man went missing. After the garbage collection scow, Ana Marie, returned to port, another man disappeared just before his imminent arrest on suspicion of murder. Only he really knows what happened that night, and why. This is a summary of the maritime report into the incident, located with difficulty after an extensive search of the official database ...

Summary of Independent Investigation into the Man Overboard Fatality on Board the Bougainville Registered Refuse Collection Scow *Ana Marie* in the Central Pacific Ocean

Japanese Government

Japanese Maritime Transport Safety Bureau

Marine Occurrence Investigation No. 687

Summary Final

Publication title

Summary of Independent Investigation into the Man Overboard Fatality on Board the Bougainville Registered Refuse Collection Scow *Ana Marie* in the Central Pacific Ocean.

Note: Excerpts from interviews conducted by Constable Yuji Tamoro, Piti Prefecture, with crew members of the *Ana Marie* are included in this summary report.

Prepared by

Japanese Maritime Transport Safety Bureau, 4 Chome-5 Kōmachi, Chiyoda City, Tokyo 104-0086

Purpose of Investigation

This incident is investigated in accordance with the IMO Resolution MSC 455(74), the Code of the International Standards and Recommended Practices for a Safety Investigation into a Marine Casualty or Marine Incident (Casualty Investigation Code).

The purpose of this investigation conducted by the Japanese Maritime Transport Safety Bureau is to determine the circumstances and the causes of the incident with the aim of improving the safety of life at sea and avoiding similar incidents in the future.

The conclusions and recommendations drawn in this report aim to identify the different factors contributing to the incident. They are not intended to apportion blame or liability towards any particular organization or person except so far as necessary to achieve the said purpose.

All information gained in this report has been forwarded to police authorities in the vessel's home port (Gladstone, Queensland, Commonwealth of Australia).

Meteorological Information

Around 1100hrs OTZ, 2 October, an Imperial Ocean Service (IOS) observation site on Saipan, reported sustained winds of 62 kt (114 mph) and a gust of 74 kt (137 mph). The highest measured storm surge was 2.6 meters above normal tide levels at an IOS gauge near San Vicente on Saipan. Tropical Cyclone advisories were issued on all stations at 1700hrs OTZ on 2 October.

Victim's Details

Henare (Henry) Manuel, aged 42, was an Aotearoa/New Zealand national. He was a registered skipper and had been in charge of the vessel for the previous five years. Crew members described Mr. Manuel as a competent and exacting skipper. He demanded high standards from his crew, although some crew have indicated that he could show impatience or anger at tasks not completed to his high standards.

Mr. Manuel suffered from a persistent lung ailment that could reduce him to fits of coughing, however, he was cleared during his most recent seafarers' medical examination and ruled fit for service. When last seen by crew on deck he was wearing a red wet weather jacket and black wet weather pants. It was reported that he was neither wearing a personal floatation device (pfd) nor tether line.

Summary

Ana Marie is a Refuse Collection Scow of 22 meters length. Her area of operations was the North Pacific Ocean, to the Japanese territory of Guam in the North, Marshall Islands in the east, and Fijian Islands to the south. The *Ana Marie* is part of the fleet representing the world-wide efforts at sea initiated by *The Great Clean-Up*. She makes up one of six ships belonging to Pacific Clean-up Solutions (PaCSol), and the only vessel operational at the time of the incident (the remaining five being mechanically impaired or in dry dock).

As the retrieval of seaborne refuse grew increasingly scarce during the present phase of *The Great Clean-Up*, her operations were extended to involve the seas north of the Mariana Islands. Her intrusion into these waters was the cause of one altercation between the *Ana Marie* and the Refuse

Collection Scow *Hindrance* which took place one week prior to the disappearance of Mr. Manual. According to *Ana Marie* log entries, crew of the *Hindrance* shot down a drone belonging to the *Ana Marie* (this action was not witnessed by any crew of the *Ana Marie*, and is denied by the skipper of the *Hindrance*). The two vessels drew close to each other and a shouting match ensued between Mr. Manual and the skipper of the *Hindrance*. Both vessels then departed. This incident is added to this report to emphasise the competitive nature of the industry as vessels sought the remains of this valuable resource, and to indicate the level of pressure skippers, including Mr. Manuel, are under to acquire their quota and fulfil orders.

At the time of the incident, the *Ana Marie* was in the Central Pacific 300 nautical miles north east of Guam near the Northern Mariana Islands (18°21.043N, 147°58.469E). The mission of the ship on its current voyage was the fulfilment of a contract for the Australian Space Administration for rare plastics to recycle into radio isotope-laced fuel for ship reactors. The *Ana Marie* was, at the time of the incident, running behind in schedule and two weeks late for delivery of that rare, valuable, and diminishing resource.

During the night of October 3, the skipper of the *Ana Marie* went missing. The scow was making way in heavy weather on a course bearing of 060 degrees magnetic to what he believed was a potential field of refuse. Seas were reported as very rough and winds at gale force. Mr. Manuel was last seen on deck the previous evening by the vessel's First Mate, Mr. Andrew Jensen, who was Officer of the Watch during those hours. Mr. Manuel was reported to have issued orders to First Mate Jensen before leaving the deck in the direction of his quarters.

At 0600hrs the skipper of the Refuse Collection Scow *Ana Marie*, Henare (Henry) Manuel, was reported by the First Mate as missing when he failed to answer calls to his quarters. After discovering his absence, a search of the ship was conducted and Mr. Manuel could not be located. It was noted that the clothing he was last seen wearing was also missing, and he was presumed to have fallen overboard. The First Mate immediately initiated Man Overboard (MoB) safety procedures in accordance with the Maritime Operators Safety Plan of the vessel. Current location was logged, a Mayday distress call sent, the vessel turned and search initiated.

Taking charge of the vessel, First Mate Andrew Jensen reversed course and instituted a Drifted Track Line search pattern to take into account conditions of the previous hours. This search continued during the daylight hours. At nightfall and the worsening of weather conditions, First Mate Jensen was advised by Rescue Coordination Centre, Guam, to cease search operations. Jensen then skippered the *Ana Marie* to the deep-water port of Apra Harbour in the Japanese Territory of Guam.

Sources of Evidence

The crew of the *Ana Marie* were interviewed at Apra Harbour by police authorities, represented by Constable Yuji Tamoro, in the prefecture. Each crew member provided accounts leading up to the incident, and of the subsequent search which took place the following day. A full transcript of interviews conducted can be located in the Full Report.

Crew interviewed:

Able Seaman, Samuel Rogers

Able Seaman, Walter Chrisp

Able Seaman, Benjamin Stuart

First Mate (Acting Skipper), Andrew Jensen

Other sources of evidence (not included in this summary): Copies of relevant ship's documentation were obtained including deck logbook entries, position information, INMARSAT-C distress messages from the ship, vessel operating procedures, statutory vessel survey records, weather report provided by Northern Mariana Observatory, and rescue report provided by Rescue Coordination Centre Guam (RCCG, Japan).

References: International Convention for the Safety of Life at Sea, 2067, and its Protocol of 2088 (SOLAS), the International Maritime Organization.

Excerpts of Interview Transcripts (transcribed audio recordings). Interviews conducted by Constable Yuji Tamoro, Piti Prefecture.

Excerpt from Interview 1: Able Seaman Samuel Rodgers

Tamoro: Mr. Rodgers, how long have you served on board the *Ana Marie*?

Rodgers: Almost six months. Just more than four, I think.

Tamoro: What were the conditions of the night that Mr. Manuel went missing?

Rodgers: They were rough. The scow was near flying off the swell. She's designed to ride the waves, which is great in big swells, but not in what we were in that night. I was down below. It wasn't my watch. I had to tie myself down to stop from flying off my bunk.

Tamoro: So, to clarify, you were not on watch, nor on deck, during the night the incident took place?

Rodgers: I just said that, didn't I?

Tamoro: Did you hear anything from your quarters during the night?

Rodgers: I heard a lot of crashing about. I mean, the scow was up and down. The storm really tossed her about (*Mr. Rodgers slapping his hands together to illustrate*). It's bad being below, but its [*expletive*] worse being up there in those conditions. It's a real [*expletive*]. Especially at night.

Tamoro: Did you hear any human sounds?

Rodgers: I heard a shout. Or more like shouting.

Tamoro: And you could differentiate these human sounds to the sounds of the storm? Of the waves, the slapping, the gear moving about?

Rodgers: It was pretty much right above me.

Tamoro: And could you identify the voices?

Rodgers: It sounded like Skipper and Jensen.

Tamoro: Sounded like?

Rodgers: It had to be. I mean, Jens was Officer of the Watch.

Tamoro: Was Mr. Jensen on watch alone?

Rodgers: No. Chrisp was with him.

Tamoro: And you are certain the voice was not from Chrisp?

Rodgers: When you hear Skipper shout, you know who it is.

Tamoro: And you would hear Mr. Manuel shout frequently?

Rodgers: Only at those that deserved it. You heard him shout at Jens *quite* a lot.

Tamoro: Can you describe the relationship between Mr. Manuel and Mr. Jensen.

Rodgers: Now you're asking the right questions. Jens and Skipper were always clashing. Jens was a know it all. Thought he knew how to do things better. I don't even think he wanted to be out there. They argued that day about turning back. God only knows why Skipper made him First Mate.

Tamoro: The meteorological records show evidence of a storm of gale force 10. Did First Mate Jensen want to turn back because of that?

Rodgers: I don't know. All I know is that they argued, again. Jens thinking he knew better.

Tamoro: And yet the scow didn't turn back, and Mr. Manuel was lost at sea.

Rodgers: All Skipper wanted was loyalty, and Jens never showed it. Now Skipper is dead. You're a cop, right? Why is that guy not behind bars? He killed Skipper. There's no way Skipper could have fallen overboard. If you knew him, you'd know that too. It was like his feet were glued to the [*expletive*] deck. No way a storm could shake him loose. Why aren't you arresting that [*expletive*] Jensen?

Tamoro: The purpose of this investigation is not to ascertain blame, nor make accusations. It is merely to collect data for further examination. All information will be forwarded to both Maritime and Police authorities in your home port. One last question: The communications log shows that Mr. Manual was under a great deal of pressure from PaCSol headquarters to fill the hold as soon as possible and return to home port with a delivery. My question is … do you think that, um, his disappearance was deliberate? An act of self—

Rodgers: No way. That's the stupidest thing I've heard yet. You know who did this. Why don't you arrest him?

Excerpt from Interview 2*:* Able Seaman Walter Chrisp

Tamoro: You were on watch during the time that Mr. Manuel is presumed to have fallen overboard?

Chrisp: That's right. We pulled night watch. Jens and me.

Tamoro: Did you hear or see Mr. Manuel at all during the night of your watch?

Chrisp: No, I wasn't on deck.

Tamoro: No? I thought you said you were on watch.

Chrisp: I was. But Jens sent me below, to the engine room.

Tamoro: Is that common practice?

Chrisp: Nothing was common practice about that night. Skipper insisted on pressing on north, despite a [*expletive*] of a storm bearing down on us. Jens tried to talk him out of it. Maybe if it came from somebody else, somebody like Rodgers who lived up Skippers [*expletive*], he might have listened. But because it was Jens talking sense, Skipper couldn't hear.

Tamoro: Is it unusual to not be on deck during your watch?

Chrisp: Not on a night like that. Being on deck would have been ridiculous. Jens sent me down, saying the same thing, that it was a hazard, a … 'unnecessary risk', is how he phrased it. So, he sent me down to monitor the engine, which was running hard out just to keep us heading forward. He's a good officer. He stayed on deck because he was Officer of the Watch. He didn't want to, but Skipper ordered a watch, so he kept it.

Tamoro: Did Mr. Jensen disagree often with Mr. Manuel?

Chrisp: Skipper had it in for him, that was pretty obvious. I think Jens sometimes encouraged that too.

Tamoro: Encouraged?

Chrisp: It's like this. If Skipper was shouting at Jens, ranting or raving at him, it meant he wasn't taking it out on me. Or any other crew. Like Ben. That's the kind of officer Jens was. He ran cover for us.

Tamoro: There are several books in Mr. Jensen's' quarters—

Chrisp: So, you've rummaged through our stuff?

Tamoro: As part of this investigation, it is our duty to examine the vessel thoroughly. There are several historical books, notably about a ship called the *Bounty*.

Chrisp: Jens was a bit of history buff. He read a lot.

Tamoro: And did he speak about his readings?

Chrisp: 'course he did. Watches are long and you gotta talk about something.

Tamoro: The story of the *Bounty* is one of a mutiny, correct?

Chrisp: It's in the title. Why are you asking me that?

Tamoro: Did Mr. Jensen ever speak about mutiny?

Chrisp: When he was talking about the *Bounty*. Which he did a lot, because that was what he was reading.

Tamoro: And about the *Ana Marie*? Did he speak of mutiny?

Chrisp: (*Laughs and shakes his head in the negative*).

Tamoro: What did Mr. Jensen speak about, when he spoke of the *Bounty*?

Chrisp: The First Mate. He thought Christian was a good one, but weak. He said First Mates were often put in very difficult situations, especially if the Captain was a first-class [*expletive*].

Tamoro: And in what way did Mr. Jensen think that Mr. Christian was weak? You need to explain, as I am not overly familiar with the story of the *Bounty*.

Chrisp: Bligh, the captain of the *Bounty*, was an outright tyrant. Jens thought he was also a bit unhinged. Christian bore the brunt of Bligh's outburst and punishments—

Tamoro: To protect his crewmates?

Chrisp: Yeah, that's what Jens thought. But eventually Christian and the crew snapped, so they mutinied and kicked the captain off the ship.

Tamoro: That does not sound weak.

Chrisp: Yeah, right? But they later hunted down the mutineers, because Bligh lived. Christian let him live, along with his followers. And Bligh returned to hunt them down. First lesson of mutiny, Jens says: kill the captain.

Tamoro: Mr. Jensen said you should kill the ship's captain?

Chrisp: [*expletive*]! No! That's not what I'm saying! He was talking about a [*expletive*] book! If you saw how hard Jens looked for Skipper that next day, there's no way you could think he could do that. I'm not saying the two were buddies. But Jens immediately took command when we couldn't find Skipper on board, issued orders without missing a beat. He turned the scow around, man. Anybody else wouldn't have dared, 'cause it could have capsized the scow. It damn near did, too, but Jens was always one step ahead, knowing what was coming and what to do before it happened. He only called off the search when your people ordered him to!

Tamoro: Some historiographers claim that, as you mention Jensen saying, Fletcher Christian was indeed weak, that he, um, 'lacked a backbone', if I have the English correct. Some claim he was manipulated by the of crew, that his Captain was not only supportive of his career, but was a friend. Captain Bligh made Mr. Christian his First Mate, just as Mr. Manuel made Mr. Jensen First Mate. Some even maintain that Christian suffered mental health issues. Can you describe the mental condition of First Mate Andrew Jensen?

Chrisp: I thought you weren't familiar with the story.

Tamoro: Can you answer the question?

Chrisp: Of course, I can. Jens was upright. He wasn't manipulated by anyone. And he always knew what he was doing. Are we done here?

Tamoro: Thank you, Mr. Chrisp, yes. It is not my role to assign responsibility of the incident, merely to investigate. One more question. In your opinion, do you think it possible for Mr. Manuel to have killed himself?

Chrisp: [*Laughter*] Not at all. He was far too stubborn for that.

Excerpt from Interview 3: Able Seaman Benjamin Stuart

Tamoro: What can you tell me of the night Mr. Manuel went missing?

Stuart: Nothing much. It was a hell of a sea. After my watch I went below to my bunk and fell asleep about as fast as my head hit the pillow.

Tamoro: And you heard nothing during the night?

Stuart: Like I said, I was out. I didn't hear anything until Jens was waking me up to start looking for Skipper.

...

Tamoro: Do you have anything to add? About the decision to carry on? The relationship between Mr. Manuel and Mr. Jensen?

Stuart: No. It's not my place to get involved with officers.

Tamoro: Did you see anything that may have led you to believe that Mr. Manuel would have deliberately fallen overboard?

Stuart: If you knew Skipper, you would know that he would rather throw all of us overboard before he ever considered himself.

Tamoro: Thank you. I need to explore all possibilities in this investigation. Is there anything you can add will help with the investigation into the incident?

Stuart: I don't have anything to add.

Excerpt from Interview 4: First Mate Andrew Jensen

Tamoro: Mr. Jensen, you were the last to see Mr. Manuel alive, is that correct?

Jensen: As far as I know, yes, I was.

Tamoro: Why was Mr. Manuel on deck during your watch?

Jensen: I don't know. Perhaps to check the vessel one last time before he turned in.

Tamoro: And what did he see?

Jensen: He saw line strewn across the deck. He was very upset about it, and he let me know—

Tamoro: By shouting at you?

Jensen: That's exactly how he let me know.

Tamoro: And what did you do, in response?

Jensen: I tidied all the line.

Tamoro: What was Mr. Manuel wearing at the time?

Jensen: He was wearing his wet weather gear. Red jacket and black pants.

Tamoro: And personal floatation device or tether line?

Jensen: Skipper never wore those. At all.

Tamoro: Were you wearing a personal floatation device and tether?

Jensen: Of course, I was. All the crew, at least when they were on my watch, wore them.

Tamoro: Your watch, Able Seaman Chrisp. Where was he at the time Mr. Manuel was on deck?

Jensen: He was in the engine room. I ordered him down to keep an eye on the engines, and get him out of the storm.

Tamoro: You raised the alarm of Mr. Manuel's absence six hours later. Why the delay?

Jensen: I don't understand what you mean by 'delay'. I was kept very busy by the storm, and when my watch ended and I handed over the deck, I was exhausted. So, I caught a couple hours sleep.

Tamoro: And Mr. Manuel was not on the next watch?

Jensen: The skipper doesn't take a watch. A skipper has to be above that, to keep a clear overview of the ship at all times. I went to Skipper's cabin to wake him for breakfast and coffee. He didn't answer, so I entered his cabin and found it empty. I checked the head, and other parts of the scow. When I couldn't find him anywhere, I ordered all hands to search. When they, too, couldn't find Skipper, I initiated MoB safety procedures.

Tamoro: Do you think it possible Mr. Manuel deliberately fell overboard?

Jensen: I have no idea. Maybe. He was pretty stressed about the contract.

Tamoro: Your actions during the emergency were logged in meticulous detail. Your search was very professional.

Jensen: Thank you. MoB is a very serious situation.

Tamoro: The logs show that you held a MoB drill with your watch just two days prior.

Jensen: Like I said, MoB is very a serious matter. And Maritime Law requires crew be regularly drilled in emergency procedures.

Tamoro: One last question, Mr. Jensen. Did you like your skipper, Mr. Manuel?

Jensen: It doesn't matter if I liked him or not. I had a job to do so I endeavoured to do it. It's about the ship, not the people.

Tamoro: But can you answer my question?

Jensen: I just did.

Conclusions and Recommendations

The report concludes that:

- The missing crew member fell overboard during a period of unsettled weather.

- The crew member is missing at sea and presumed dead.

- The crew member was not wearing a personal floatation device or safety tether line.

- There are no conclusive findings as to why the crew member was on deck nor how or why he fell overboard.

- The skipper of the vessel was under considerable pressure from the employing company, Pacific Clean-up Solutions (PaCSol) to complete contracted delivery of refuse which may have influenced his decision to sail northwards during storm conditions.

The report recommends that:

- Safety procedures onboard the *Ana Marie* be reassessed and revised to ensure safety of crew while at sea, such as mandatory wearing of personal floatation devices and tether lines during night and/or unsettled conditions, regardless of rank or role on ship.

- *Ana Marie* undergoes thorough re-inspection by Maritime Safety personnel before cleared for further sea duty.

- Authorities continue to investigate the testimony of crew members of the *Ana Marie* in order to clarify any discrepancies in their accounts of the night in question and events leading up to the disappearance of the skipper.

- This report strongly recommends that crew of the *Ana Marie* be detained in their home port (Gladstone, Queensland) until police authorities are completely satisfied that none of the crew played a role in the disappearance and presumed death of their skipper, Henare (Henry) Manuel.

Benthic Material

As the narrator describes, benthic material is found on the ocean floor. In this story, he tells some trainees what got hauled up ...

"Weirdest thing I ever caught?"

Of course, they would ask that. They just spent a whole day on non-quota by-catch. Corals, sponges, plants, molluscs, wood, rocks. Anything that the net of a bottom trawler hauls up with its catch has to be recorded. Bottom trawling can be very harmful to the sea floor, so all the pictures and notes they'll be taking are a part of trying to mitigate that.

Stories abound. One of the most popular involves a washing machine. It's illegal to dump any rubbish into the ocean, so the fishing boat had to take the rusty, scum encrusted thing with them and land it with the rest of their catch.

"It's okay," the government fishery observer told the skipper. "It won't count as part of your quota." Funny guy, if it ever, really, happened.

"That will cost you another pint," I answered.

They burst out laughing as a trainee arrived at that exact moment with a tray full of pints. He placed one in front of me, a tall guy who said his name was Mike, but everybody called Tree. Now I was stuck. I nodded my thanks to Tree, picked up the pint and took a sip. I lost count of drinks. The empties were cleared away far too fast in this pub. Three? Four? Sailors are known for having a terrible relationship with alcohol. They are dry for weeks while at sea, but get mind shatteringly wasted when on ground. I wasn't one of those. At least, I didn't want to be. I was merely visiting here, down for a day to cover some material on their course. This was almost like a holiday, of sorts, so a few drinks couldn't hurt.

They were a good cohort. They got on well together and took in most of what was delivered. And, as they hadn't been to sea yet, they were hungry for anything an experienced observer had to tell them. They'll learn most of the job on their first trip, going out with another observer and shadowing them for weeks. Most of what we teach them on land is just the government covering it's ass. Observers are their most 'at risk' employees. They board a fishing vessel and go hundreds of miles off shore, watching and recording what is caught, ensuring the company keeps to their limit, testing the health of the fish caught. And recording anything that isn't a fish that happens to wind up in the net.

"Weirdest thing! Come on!" the loud, young one named Zac called.

He's going to have to reign it in on board if he wants to have a good time, but he seems quite socially astute. He can read what is appropriate, what isn't, and when. I'm sure he'll be fine. I take another drink and wait for the chatter at the end of the table to die out. The beer in this town tastes too good. I have definitely had too much.

"Weirdest thing I ever caught," I repeated for dramatic effect. "You know, I didn't catch anything. I was just there to observe others catching—"

"Come on! You know what we mean!" Zac said.

So, I told them. It was my sixth or seventh trip out. I was getting into the groove of the lifestyle. Six or eight weeks out, then as long ashore as I wanted, with a fat pay check waiting. The first year I chased those pay days, and kept signing up for another trip a week or two after returning. Every international ship was required by law to have an observer on board, and most national ones in vulnerable fisheries did too, so there was never a shortage of work. I sailed on the Russian ships, eating at the captain's table. I sailed on the Korean, with their Indonesian crews. We got a three-hundred-dollar budget on those for 'stores', which meant comfort food that Russians or Koreans just don't have. Part of being 'at risk' is being looked after, so a usually tight-fisted Ministry was generous for a change.

It was on a Korean vessel. I can't remember the name, and couldn't tell you anyway. Confidentiality and all that. You have to learn to be careful about talking about your job. What ship you're on, where they fished, what you thought about them. You have to keep it to yourself.

The trainees are all given an article that appeared in the *Herald*. A reporter rode along with a Russian fishing vessel, and not being able to speak the language turned to the one Kiwi on board, the fisheries observer. The result was a very interesting article, and an observer promptly losing their job. Sounds harsh, but we're talking about commercially sensitive practices, and a relationship between industry and government built on trust. You don't talk to the press unless cleared. You don't mess with that trust.

I didn't know if I would like the Korean boats. The factories below decks have lower ceilings, so there is no grate between your gum boots and the water sloshing over the deck. They eat different foods. They adhere to a hierarchy. On a Kiwi boat you might eat anywhere in the mess. On a Korean boat, you're considered a junior officer and must dress and act like it. That means eating at the captain's table. The Indonesian only crew eat after the Korean officers, and you, are finished.

I actually liked their order. And I may be soft, but the food on the captain's table was better than what the crew ate. The only thing I spent a chunk of that three hundred dollars on was fresh ground coffee. My cabin reeked of it. It wasn't that bad at all—except for the swaying back and forth, the occasional bout of sea sickness, and the ever-present smell of fish.

It was a big haul. The fishing master had set the net at a beautiful location. The net surfaced and my first 'eyeball estimate' was that it was a lot. I was going to have my work cut out for me on this one. I made sure I had my camera, my notepad, and pencils to spare. The winches slowly dragged the net on board and I could see they hit a motherload of orange roughy. But there was bound to be a large by-catch impact. As the net continued to be brought aboard, I noticed a large bulge in the middle. For all I knew, it could have been a washing machine, or a protected species like a basking shark, so I waited as the net was lifted and emptied into the pound, the stainless-steel tanks that hold the catch until it's processed in the factory below.

Only the bulge didn't shift. Fish streamed around it, but it stayed where it was. When the net was empty, the bulge moved, as if something was struggling inside it. Because something *was* struggling inside it. The bulge moved towards the mouth of the net, which was just above the pound. The Indonesian deckhands backed away. I backed away. We watched as the bulge made its way to the mouth, and then stepped out of the net.

It's hard to describe what it was. I feel like something has scratched away at the picture in my mind, because that's probably what happened. It was about a metre and a half tall, standing on legs, with arms moving angrily beside it. I use the terms legs and arms and angry because they seem to fit, not because they're accurate. It had a head, of sorts, and a mouth, or at least a breathing hole, that sucked in air in wet gasps. It had eyes, I'm sure of that. It turned its head and scanned the deck and all of us standing on it. I don't think calling it an 'it' is appropriate, but I don't know what else to use. It was definitely a *something*, but I don't know what. Its eyes met mine and I literally staggered back a step.

Then it spoke. I mean, it made sounds out of what might have been a mouth. I jumped when it did. The Indonesian deck hands jumped as well, so I know they heard it, whatever they said after. And I know they understood what it was saying, same as me.

It was clear it wasn't happy.

"What the fuck are you assholes doing!"

I stood there, mouth open, totally frozen on the spot. I heard shouting in Indonesian, heard a crash as, I assumed, a deck hand or two were stumbling backward and falling over, trying to get as far from what they caught as possible. I should have been doing the same, but like I said, I just couldn't move. It took a step towards me, waving what I think was an arm.

"I come to this speck of a planet to visit the only really sentient type of life it has, and you dumb fucks run a rake through it!"

If it wanted an answer, I couldn't give it. I think I even wet myself. It took another step towards me and pointed at my chest as if it were a target.

"You! Dumb! Fucks!" The words sounded like distant thunder, a growing rumble that promised so much more.

Then it spread its arms, or whatever they were, as wide as they could go. I don't know how, some sort of intuition, but I had an idea of what it was going to do with those arms. So, I did all I could do. I fell to the deck, assumed the foetal position, closed my eyes as tight as I could, and put my hands over my ears.

I can only guess that it clapped its hands together because I didn't see. The deck shook, and even with my eyes closed, I felt blinded by a flash of light. I felt myself slide backward across the trawl deck until I hit the rail. I stayed curled up right there for I don't know how long, until a deck hand eventually shook me by the shoulder. He shook for quite a while. I finally opened my eyes to see all of the Indonesians standing over and looking down at me. One, the only one that knew some English, bent a knee and felt my head.

"You okay?" he asked.

I jerked away from him, trying to scramble farther away from the net, but I was already as far I could get without running through a hatch. My eyes must have been the size of saucers as I looked up and down the deck.

It was empty.

"Where is it? Where is it?" I kept asking, and the deck hand's face looked more and more worried.

"Where is what?" he asked.

I must have continued asking the same question, because he stopped trying to reach me. I remember being lifted off the deck, carried through the passage and into my quarters. I remember the Korean mate, who was also the ship's medic, sliding a needle into me. Then I don't remember anything for quite a while.

When I woke up, it seemed that the crew didn't remember anything either, just that the observer seemed to have some sort of breakdown on deck during a haul. My talking about the by-catch only seemed to reinforce that. They put up with me for the rest of trip, but I've never been given a Korean ship since.

My pint was empty, but nobody got up to refill it. They all sat there, staring, waiting for more, waiting for an explanation or something, some sort of resolution, or at least a punch line. But there wasn't any.

The Irish one, Rachel, looked at me with a particularly Irish smirk. I'm sure she thought I just described a leprechaun and am probably making fun of her. She doesn't think it's true, what I saw.

Close Encounter

First contact, or any alien contact, is usually told with dramatic or fantastical story. But what if it happens more often than thought, and in a much more intimate fashion? Perhaps like in this instance, somewhere in the Southern Ocean ...

The choice is easy this time. On a planet made up two thirds of water, the desire is strong to explore that vast wetness. And who better to travel with than one of its largest and most majestic species, itself a fellow traveller? The choice, of course, is subjective. There is an attraction to its smooth white feathers and elegant large wings. Entering this vessel feels like a homecoming. Its consciousness makes willing room, giving a comfortable place to nestle besides. Together, we move as one.

The ocean spreads around us; an undulating body decorated with white froth. Swell builds, forming hillocks to a horizon stretching three hundred and sixty degrees. Everywhere its eyes search is water, and yet it is home. Although ever changing, it is familiar here. With wings outstretched and locked in place, we glide effortlessly. A gust of wind finds us and without thought, the slightest movement of feathers keeps our body balanced and on course. But on course for where? The feeling of home, of responsibility, and yes, a feeling of love.

Such emptiness. Such beauty. A wing dips, and we turn and descend. Water rushes to greet us, but we turn and glide in a new direction. And then we level, sea skimming beneath us. A slight tension of muscle, an imperceptible adjustment of feathers, and we soar, only to dip and turn again. It is playing, it is showing off, but with purpose. Pink, webbed feet leave the warmth of tail feathers. Sea approaches, wings pull in and feet gently slap the surface, skim for the briefest moment, and we sit on the surface, held by an endless hand. We know this hand well. It is home. We ride waves, up and down, to summit and then to valley.

And with a deft movement of beak, we feed. Again, and again, in frenzy and yet in no hurry, we turn and submerge and kick into the depths and our yellow tipped beak seeks out a flash and acquires it. We are filled with an inner warmth. We are not merely eating for ourselves. We surface and repeat until we are full, until, with a slight flick of wings, we begin to lift. Webbed feet step on water. One step, two steps, three and we are again in the air, our home. Tendons lock and currents carry. Hours pass, and oranges and pinks soften the horizon. The sun continues on its own journey, ever westward, but we carry on as stars emerge. With my gentle prompting, eyes gaze at the distant suns around which circle distant worlds, and it knows from where its guest has come.

The sky is again filled with colour, this time from the east. We follow a familiar smell, the smell of land. Sounds greet us. It is a chorus of life. Wings adjust, speed diminishes, our heart beats rapidly in anticipation, and there! Wide feet slap on soft earth. Climbing atop a mound of soil and vegetation we smell home and mate and future. Beak greets beak, our heart swells. Youngling reaches with open beak and we share our bounty carried within. We sit in the warmth of home, until it is time for one to move on and visit others.

The Bardo

An alien is caught in the web of life surrounding planet Earth ...

Taan wrestled with the controls, but couldn't stop the spin. He had gotten too close, drawn by an unimaginable force, and his will was too weak. He wanted to see, to touch, to explore—every part of his being drawn to the blue green sphere. It vibrated with a force that was irresistible. He knew the risk, as well as the danger, but it wasn't enough to avoid the trap. The bioshphere pulsed around the globe, the life contained within reaching out like solar flares, grasping and inviting, and drawing down to the fertile planet below. And it reached out and grabbed Taan, who got too close because his will was too weak, and the planet was too strong.

As he fell, his view became a blur of black space and turbulent cloud, switching places too quickly as he overcorrected. He tried to slow his spin, his descent, his trajectory, but over corrected more. He felt his body shift with the inertia, pinning him to one side of the cockpit. He felt consciousness begin to dim, a faint darkening in the corner of his vision. Fighting to maintain focus, he forced the controls, but the spin didn't slow. His world become white as his ship plummeted through cloud, and then the surface emerged. Spinning colours was all he saw, white, and green, and blues. The controls were useless, but he continued to pull on them. The clouds became more distant and the green closer. Taan tried to keep his eyes open as his ship crashed in a blinding explosion on the surface the waiting planet.

Taan opened his eyes after days of darkness. He sought out familiar warmth and wiggled with those around him, all competing for the nourishing liquid. There was enough for all. His mouth opened and closed until it latched onto the pink nipple. He was consumed with a hunger that was never sated, and he drank hungrily. Only when his small stomach was full and a sleepy contentment overwhelmed him did he think of the stars, of a distant home, of a ship spinning, of a name. *I have a name!* he thought, but sleep came and he forgot.

Over days he grew in size and strength. His eyes became sharp, for what lay close to his whiskers. His nose guided him to other scents, to seeds and crumbs and exciting opportunities. He explored farther, sometimes with his siblings, but more frequently alone. He kept to the shadows because danger lurked in the light. It lurked in the air above. It lurked around corners. Danger was everywhere, so he moved fast. He moved fast in his dreams, images that made less and less sense, clouds and greens and blues and danger. Taan twitched his nostrils and followed a delicious smell. He was drawn forward, as if the smell was reaching for him, grasping and inviting. *A beautiful planet!* Taan thought, though the words carried no meaning.

His eyes fixed on the prize that his nose had won for him. His mouth watered and his feet carried him towards the yellow cube. He opened his jaws and joyously bit into the prize and heard the snap of the trap that crushed his back.

Taan saw white and green and blue white and green and blue and fire and dark and yellow and warmth and milk and then all was darkness.

Taan was trapped. His secure and comforting shelter was now claustrophobic. Suffocating. He pushed against it with weak feet and legs. His back was too fragile to wedge against the walls. So, he swung his head forward, striking his prison with the middle of his face. He struck again, and again, only resting when his efforts were finally rewarded with a crack in his prison. There was a way out, a possibility of escape, of regaining control and returning home. He had to get home, and he was trapped. He pecked again, he used his frail body, and the walls around him began to crumble.

Taan emerged cold and naked and blind, but warm soft feathers soon surrounded him. He worked his head free and opened his mouth, an instinct, nothing more, and a hard beak stuffed food deep into his throat. He swallowed and felt another sensation, hunger. His mouth opened again and again, demanding more, and more was given.

Over days, he grew. His naked skin began to be covered, and his eyes received light, slowly focussing on his surroundings. Sometimes he was left alone, and he felt alone and far from home, even though he was home. During these times he opened his arms, arms that seemed light enough to hold the air. He knew somehow that one day they would and he would fly. He knew he flew before, and he would again. Soon. He also knew he had a name, but he could not remember what it was.

But Taan never did fly. He was alone, again, his parents seeking food for his growing body, when he heard a rustle nearby. He made himself still and small, but he was hunted by smell, not movement or sight, and his scent was captured. As the approaching noise grew louder, he made himself as large as he could, spreading his frail arms and opening his mouth wide, protesting as loudly as he could. It was a mere squawk, and it was quickly silenced when sharp teeth crushed the bones of his frail head.

Taan saw white and green and blue and white and green and blue and fire and dark and yellow and warmth and milk and food stuffed deep into him and then all was darkness.

Taan cried as jagged air streamed into his raw and unused lungs. Again and again, it burned him inside. His eyes burned in the glare, even when closed as tightly as possible. All warmth escaped. He was naked and blinded and helpless. Taan cried more, and his lungs burn worse. Finally, he was covered and moved and placed on a living bed of warmth, a warm he knew because he shared it before. He smelled the warmth and opened his mouth, searching with lips, as if possessed by a spell. They closed around the warmth and he suckled, filling his mouth, his throat, his belly, and he had no name or home other than this one, at this moment.

The Originals

They thought they had found a planet for free, uninhabited. All that remained as evidence of past occupants were overgrown ruins. But what happened to those that were there before? A ship is sent to investigate. Finally catching up with the original inhabitant's generation ship, they find out ...

"It started with the *siml*." She spoke softly, her mouth near the rim of her mug.

"I don't understand that term." Donna said. Words were out and she didn't want to scare them away. "Is that a name? Of a place?" she asked, gently coaxing, her question like breadcrumbs, attracting a timid bird.

Moments passed in silence. The woman stared into her drink as if more words were hidden there. Arnil's usual state seemed to be silence. The alien put up with the anti-body tests the ship's doctor wanted to run, allowed her to use the injector to complete another battery of immunisations. She understood the importance of the tests prior to returning to her disc, or waking the crew to flip the Seed Ship. It was clear she realised that she was now, in a way, contaminated, and that it was unsafe for her to return until this human was certain she was protected, and they knew how to protect the others sleeping. Her own role was that of a doctor to her people, which was why she was woken first. She listened to all of the human doctor's explanations, absorbing every detail, only asking the rare question for clarification. It had mostly been a one-way conversation to this point as the human tried to explain why they were here, where they came from, and what they wanted.

The human couldn't imagine how she would react if the situation were reversed. To lose so much! When exploratory ships first came across the ocean planet, they claimed it as their own. Convoys of colony ships brought settlers by the thousands, and they occupied the many island chains dotting the globe. It was the first inhabitable planet humanity had discovered in over one hundred years of searching. They built new cities and farms and factories next to the ruins of those that lived there first. But those people, whoever or whatever they were, were long gone. They left only remnants of a long-lost civilization. A generation later, a xeno-archeologists found traces of data, pieces of a distant past, a name the Originals called themselves: Ruan. They also found evidence in the data of a Seed Ship, a spore of the ancient people cast out into space, for reasons unknown.

The ship was still out there, the researchers argued, slowly crossing the empty expanse in search of a new start. The math couldn't lie—the numbers were the path leading the way. With the promise of advanced alien technology an earth-based consortium backed the project to hunt down and retrieve the vessel. They built the Step Ship *Chōgenbō*, able to harness the power of a sun to fold space, to cross vast distances in moments rather than centuries. Stepping removed the distance between points A and B by putting both points in the same place. Rather than taking generations to cross the expanse, the *Chōgenbō* simply stepped across it.

Greed was the base motivation of the major backers, the promise of what they could make from alien technology. Most of the crew had higher motives. It was possible survivors of the alien civilization were still alive. So, it was in part a humanitarian mission, for lack of an appropriate name or detailed knowledge of who they were trying to save. The search took months, but the *Chōgenbō* finally caught the ship as it sped towards another star, which it might reach in another millennium. It was massive, five discs each holding twenty thousand frozen Originals in cryopods. The discs connected by a central chamber and powered by multiple fusion reactors. The crew of the *Chōgenbō* woke one of 'the originals' to explain the plan: wake enough crew to help them flip and decelerate the vessel. Once stopped, they would attach the *Chōgenbō* to the massive ship, and Step with them back to their home world.

Now Donna was sitting with one of the Originals.

"A name, yes," Arnil answered. "This device is improving, but it is still very lacking." She glanced at the translator badge pinned to her tunic before returning her gaze back to her drink.

"But not of a place. No," she laughed, or what Donna was beginning to recognise as a show of humour. "*Siml* are small creatures. Were. They are … were … everywhere. Pests. They burrow under gardens, chew into walls. Dirty animals. They multiply if unchecked."

"They sound like mice," Donna offered.

"That is a word with no reference," Arnil said. "What is a mice?"

"Not a mice … mice is more than one, plural," Donna said. "A *mouse* is a small mammal. It can fit into the palm of a hand, covered with short fur, small ears. It can be quite cute. But they breed rapidly, and can infest a home. They can cause damage, even spread disease."

"A *siml* is bigger," Arnil said, setting her mug down on the table. "A *siml* can fit in my palm," she said, opening her large hand.

"That sounds more like a rat," Donna said.

"That is a word with no reference."

"A rat is like a mouse," Donna said. "Only bigger and uglier. And dirty. Sharp teeth, carries bugs, germs that infect humans, zoonotic diseases."

"Maybe a *siml* is like a raat then," Arnil said. She took a drink from her mug. "They started to disappear. Nobody knows when it started. Something that isn't liked, that hides and doesn't want to be seen, is hard to notice when it is no longer there."

Donna picked up the flask and indicated to Arnil's cup. She poured more coffee after Arnil's cheek twitched. Only through careful observation, and a little experimentation, did she learn that gesture and its meaning.

"The smell," Arnil said. "Dead and rotting *siml*. In wall cavities, under walkways. Most were pleased at the discovery. A disease that eradicates a pest." Arnil shook her head. "Stupid *Fonnen*."

That is word with no reference, Donna thought, but filed it away to ask about later. She smiled at Arnil, letting her continue.

"By that time other mammals were dying," Arnil said. "Mostly small animals, in the bush. Untamed mammals. Again, it was the smell that alerted us. The disease had spread from the *siml*, and was infecting other animals. Only when their precious *merendt* started to die did they begin to think there was a problem. And even then, it took far too long for them to realise what was really happening."

"I am sorry," Donna thought it safe to interject. "But you said a word. *Merendt*. Can you describe that for me?"

"A *merendt* is a mammal that lives inside, where Ruan sleep and eat. It is a disgusting practice." Arnil turned her long, narrow face towards Donna. "Imagine! A mammal treading where you sit, where you eat, even where you sleep! Giving them names! Would you have a mammal walking freely in your sick bay?"

"That would be unsanitary," Donna said.

"Precisely! These *fonnen* with their *merendt*," she shook her head. "*Merendt* that hunt *siml*, eat them, bring them inside. Idiots!"

Donna turned her head and spoke into the translator pinned to her uniform. "Add to dictionary: *merendt*, pet." She faced Arnil. That's close enough for now, she thought. Peter, the xeno-linguist, can work on the vocabulary later, and hopefully the problem with conjunctions. She brought up the other word. "And *Fonnen*? What is that?"

Donna recognised the glint in Anril's eyes as the Ruan version of a smile. "It is a name for those living in the north. Not a real name. They don't call themselves that. They don't like it."

"I am learning Ruan slang!" Donna said.

Arnil jolted as Donna laughed. She was still not used to the strange sounds human make when they find amusement.

Donna noticed the subtle flinch and stopped. "I am so sorry," she said. "There is nothing funny about this." Donna looked down briefly, ashamed of her outburst. To Arnil, these events were measured in months, not centuries.

"It is oh-kay," Arnil said, trying out human slang. "There are no more *Fonnen* to be offended."

Donna pursed her lips, no doubt another expression that would confuse her guest. The human face had almost four times more muscles than the Ruan. They must look like they are constantly spasming and out of control.

"It started in the north?" Donna asked, attempting to steer the conversation back to its beginning. "With the *siml*, in the north?"

Arnil picked up her mug, took a sip, started to lower it again but stopped, transfixed by the black liquid. "Yes," she said. "It started in the north."

Arnil watched the growing catastrophe, like those around her, not really aware that that was what it was. Not aware at the beginning, anyway. Stories from the northern archipelagos of rodents dying. Mass die offs. She watched the information feeds, programs reporting happenings, which always finished with clips meant to amuse or reassure the viewer. No matter what was covered—natural disasters, political intrigues, technological developments—these short clips reassured the viewer all was not bad or boring. The *siml* dying off. What could be bad about that?

Arnil didn't know why that particular story burned into her memory. It was just moments long, a few images of emaciated pests. She could vividly bring up the image of the announcer. The humour in his eyes as he joked about the benefit. Maybe on a much deeper level she knew there was nothing good about the news, much as she disliked the creature. Nothing just dies. There is always a reason. Something to cause it. Her colleagues at the clinic agreed, and they followed the progress of the *siml* disease, as it was called in the beginning. It seemed to be able to jump water, appearing on nearby islands, with no obvious means of transmission. *Siml* do not swim, and they are usually detected when trying to stow away on a sea vessel.

Some argued that the disease might be natural. As if nature were ridding itself of an entire species. There were extinctions in the past, whether caused by climate change, cataclysmic events, or Ruan themselves. If the *siml* could not adapt, then they deserved their fate. They were no longer fit to share the planet.

But Arnil didn't want to believe that. Her training prevented it. And then the disease leapt to other mammals, and that theory was dropped. Bush mammals were found, emaciated and rotting.

Some of the larger species even shuffled into settlements, staggering in their weakened state, their muzzles distorted in confusion and pain. Those creatures were dispatched and burned. Some were studied, but little was discovered.

When the *merendt* of the northerners began to die the stories moved up in the information programs. To Arnil, it seemed that the *Fonnen* cared more about their *pets* than their younglings, which of course, was not true. Fear began to infect communities. Although, when island authorities started issuing edicts forbidding the practice of having *merendt* inside their homes, it was surprising how many continued to disobey.

The jump to *merendt* continued to other domesticated mammals. Resource mammals, used for foods, for clothing, for industry. It affected stomachs and livelihoods, so more began to take notice. Exports from affected islands were halted, but the cause didn't stop. It continued to hop from island to island, until the entire archipelago of *Yondrta* was infected.

As with the *siml*, as with every species that it touched, the disease was ruthless and efficient. Clinicians like Arnil could not understand a disease that killed all of its hosts, but that is exactly what this one did. Rather than let some of the affected survive for future infections, it chose instead to mutate and consume another species. And then another, and another.

Arnil and her colleagues hung a large map on the wall of the clinic and tracked the epidemic. As the disease spread to other mammals, they used different colours. Lines connected islands. Then they connected archipelagos. The lines became like rainbows of death, multicolour arcs crossing expanses of water. Some communities attempted to cull affected mammals, which was heart breaking as whole herds were put down, but the spread continued. The coloured lines inched their way around the globe, creeping east around the world, and slowly to the south. Towards Arnil's home island.

"It is called *Hestrilx*," Arnil said. "My home."

"Where was … *is* it located?" Donna asked, determined to avoid the past tense.

"In the temperate climes," Arnil said. "South of the tropics, away from the heat. We have more than one season, summer tempered by cooler days as the sun rests."

"What did it look like?" Donna asked, trying to place the name on the newer map of Pemako, or as Arnil knew it, Ruanae.

"It is a long island, with a strong backbone of mountains that wear a coat of white in the colder months," Arnil said wistfully. "In the summer they are ablaze with green. As the seasons change it is a joy to watch. The white recedes, retreats, as the green climbs higher and higher, as if the snows are melting in front of a green fire. My favourite time of year."

Arnil closed her eyes and sat silently. Tears slowly ran down the sides of Arnil's face. Donna already knew Ruan cried. She had cried with Arnil, the day she was woken.

"If we had this, it may have been different." Arnil gestured to the sick bay of the *Chōgenbō*. She was impressed with human's understanding of their bodies. "You have a much better understanding of medicines," Arnil said.

"Humans are much weaker than Ruan," Donna admitted. "Our bodies … need more care. So, we have devoted a great deal of time studying them. Our fallibility, our frailty, has often given us strength."

"Could you have stopped it?" Arnil asked.

Donna hesitated. The bodies of the Ruan were stronger and generally healthier than human, which meant they lived longer, with less illness. It also meant their medical sciences were under-developed and far behind that of Earth. Infections didn't manifest when Ruan skin was scratched or cut. Diseases didn't migrate from living near or with animals. The immune system would eradicate the introduced pathogen before the injured Ruan would even notice. They did not experience ailments that humans accepted as normal. Colds, flus, rashes, sexually transmitted disease were all extremely rare. Which led to complacency, rather than the age-old drive of humans to obsessively study their bodies and try to find out why it broke down so easily.

Donna had studied past pandemics. Rome was brought to its knees by a pandemic, and the ancient world probably never really recovered from it. To the Ruan, the Romans would have appeared stone age ignoramuses playing around a small pond. But they survived sickness. The Antonine Plague was brought back to Rome by soldiers returning from conquests in Asia. It was named after the emperor of the time, Marcus Aurelius Antonius. It killed up to five million people, twenty five percent of those it infected. It may have even had as high as a thirty five percent kill rate. Marcus Aurelius himself would be a victim. Donna compiled a list of pandemics during her research. Her list got depressingly repetitive. Plagues and flus and new viruses killing millions.

But humanity had managed to survive all of them, even find cures and vaccines, as well as scatter itself across systems to ensure the survival of the species. It survived past pandemics, when it did not have the ability to seed other planets. That, Donna reflected, may have been a bit of pure luck.

"When you were revived," Donna said, "I gave you injections to protect you from any illness we may have introduced. Any pathogens that your body did not have immunity to fight. Although your immunity may have defended you against most of them, it would not against all." Samples of *seeker* flesh were traded between consortium and university laboratories, brought from humanity's first encounter with the Ruan. Opportunities to study the two cadavers were sought after, and occasionally granted. As well as send a Seed Ship out into the expanse, in their desperation the Ruan also sent *seekers*, whose only mission was to seek out any technology that might help their species in its time of crisis. Frozen in cryo-sleep, these volunteers would only be woken when their ship's AI detected that technology. One ship finally found it, but their planet had died thousands of years before. They attacked a convoy, programming a Step to their home world before they were killed. The convoy found an abandoned paradise.

One of the *seekers* carried the viral agent that decimated its species, although there were no outward signs. Researchers debated about passive carriers, dormant germs, transmission periods, and a host of other theories. Regardless of view, they had obtained a sample of what killed the alien species. It was also accurate to say that after studying the corpses human scientists had a better understanding of Ruan physiology than the Ruan themselves. Donna didn't say it, but she suspected Arnil knew.

"We would have used an anti-viral treatment," she said instead. "One similar to antidotes developed during the pandemics of the Decline, prior to the Great Awakening on Earth. Unfortunately, we have had a great deal of experience with disease." *A simple anti-viral that would have protected your people,* she thought.

Arnil looked around the sick bay, at the clean work surfaces and instrumentations she was only just becoming familiar with. The human taught her how to use the electron microscope that allowed her to see the individual atoms within cells. No foreign invader could hide from the eyes of these aliens, no matter how small or how buried in the flesh it might be. *Yes, this technology could have saved the Ruan,* Arnil thought. *But you were not here when we needed it.*

"It doesn't matter," she said.

"It does matter," Donna said. "It means your people will be protected when they return to Ruanae."

"My people," Arnil repeated. "We don't even know exactly when the first began to die," she said after a pause. "It was only when … this is very difficult."

Something began to itch at the back of Arnil's mind as she and her colleagues drew the coloured lines on the map. As new species of mammals were added to the list of infected, lines became dashes or dots, or shapes, to differentiate from the other lines as they ran out of colours to separate them. But even that practice stopped when the collection of lines grew too crowded. Nothing stopped the relentless progress. All shipping on the sea, all transport through the air, was halted. Archipelagos isolated themselves, and the islands within locked down, quarantined. Yet islands without contact of any sort still watched their mammals die.

And then the first Ruan grew ill. It was near the epicentre of the outbreak. A Guardian masked his sore muscles as long as he could, but the eating pain grew too much, consumed his pride and courage until he broke down. The disease grew throughout his musculature, wasting what was once pure strength into soft weak flesh. Others complained of pain—their arms, thighs, abdomen. Soon, like the first, they died as wasted shadows of their former selves, jaws slack and open as even their masticatory muscles degenerated. The Guardians were the strongest among the Ruan, and they were the first to fall. A wasting disease taking the pride of the species, laying waste to an entire caste.

But they were soon followed by others. A disease that took the strongest first inevitably turned to the weaker. Elders began to succumb. Younglings woke crying in pain, and by day's end were silent in death. Whereever the plague touched, no one survived.

"It is unimaginable," Donna said.

"It was a nightmare, a dream that had no waking," Arnil said. "We could only helplessly and impotently watch it progress, from land to land. We watched our mammals intently. We watched each other. We worried about every ache."

Tears ran down her long face. She let out a shuddering breath and held her head in her hands. Donna reached over and touched Arnil's shoulder, an act of sympathy and comfort, but a human act, alien to the Ruan. Arnil moved her shoulder away from the unwanted touch. She rubbed the tears from her face.

"It took time to see it," Arnil said. "We weren't the first to notice that there was a pattern in the spread." She turned and looked at Donna. "By that time the populations of whole Archipelagos were gone. Millions dead. More were dying elsewhere. For some … it did not bring out their best. No one wants to die. They tried to flee the onslaught of the disease by leaving their homelands. They took to the sky and the sea. But none would have them. These refugees were sunk, or they were shot out of the air. Many were killed. Our Guardians were weakened, dying, so others took their place. Those who were common, weaker in mind and body. It was ugly, and it was brutal. It was a time that tested our character, and we were found wanting."

"The Guardians are better than you?" Donna asked. "What do you mean?"

"Guardians do not only protect our homes and communities," Arnil said. "They protect our essence, our *xentoldt—*"

"I am sorry," Donna interrupted. "That is one of those words the translator cannot process."

"Guardians are chosen when they are younglings," Arnil said. "They are brought up in strict discipline, in special, holy places. They are taught how to fight, how to be protectors. They learn all types of combat, the use of weapons, including their hands and feet. Their physical form is very beautiful."

Again, Donna recognised the Ruan form of a smile. "But they are untouchable. They live apart, where they study the old ways. The Guardians sit in silence for hours, sometimes days, contemplating why they might fight, and when they might use their strength. I will say a word that this device may translate."

Donna heard two words, *deep* and *reflection.*

"I understand, I think," Donna said. "They are warrior monks."

Arnil bent her head forward, as she had learned was a non-verbal human way to indicate the affirmative. "Your words translate to something close. There are many conceptual words that can be used to describe what a Guardian is." Arnil had grappled with several conceptual words the aliens that woke her used. She decided that it wasn't the fault of the translation device, but that some words were layered with meaning and used in many different situations. She deactivated the device on occasion to hear some. The muscles in her tongue didn't allow her to repeat some.

"Your word," Arnil said. "Can you repeat it?"

"Love?" Donna asked.

Arnil turned off her translator, had Donna say it again, and then bent her head forward in a nod.

"Yes," she said. "The Guardians learn this and apply this in all aspects of their waking. They strive to express it in everything they do, and everything they think. It is why they are apart from the common. They take it upon themselves to maintain all that is good about the Ruan. What makes us Ruan. Our *xentoldt*. They would willingly sacrifice themselves to protect what is good in us, if that is what was required, even when, out of our weakness or hatred or greed, we do not want protection."

Arnil breathed deeply. A sigh, one of the few gestures, like tears, both species used. "When the Guardians became ill … when they succumbed … it was an unimaginable loss. There was nobody there to protect us, and we were truly lost."

"And yet they did protect you," Donna said. "They saved you. It was because of the *seekers*, the Guardians, that we found Ruanae, and that we learned of you."

"We both know that is not what happened," Arnil said. "Although their intentions were pure, they killed your people. And they were too late."

Arnil studied the map on the wall, with its coloured lines blurred into a thickening smear that covered whole swathes of the northern hemisphere. She took her earlier suspicion and married it to current speculation. Wild theories sprouted like fungi, but one made more sense than the others. Arnil searched through databases until she found what she wanted. She printed it off and took it to the wall. She held it up and studied both the large map and the smaller sheet of data. On an ocean world the winds seem to roam free, when and where they like.

But they do not. Like the ocean itself, the wind follows currents, moving across the globe in patterns. The currents flow in a circular motion over the north, until the seasons change and they wind their way south, circulating over the entire planet. Circulating the disease. The southern temperate zone was currently untouched. It wouldn't be for long.

Arnil and other clinicians rushed to sound a warning, as Elders rushed to calm panic. They were both too late. The decision to leave was made in the midst of chaos. Society was collapsing faster than the disease spread. As panic ensued, Guardians removed those in civil authority and tried to restore order themselves. But as they too sickened, order died with them. Islands were deserted, all their inhabitants dead, or desperately trying to flee. The seas filled with boats large and small, all heading south. Many disappeared under the waves as their vessels took on water, or as fights broke out, or deliberately sunk as they strayed too close to other boats. The rare islands that took them in were soon infected, by the refugees, or by the winds, none knew.

Before long, no refugee was welcome. Strangers were shot on sight. Broods locked in their dwellings fought any trying to enter, but they were still not safe, because there was no safety. Many who realised this took their own lives the moment symptoms began to manifest. Fatigue. Pain deep within the muscles. Headache. Blurring vision. They did anything to avoid the inevitable and horrendous death that waited. Early information feeds showed the victims, but that was before the producers realised that they were looking at all of their fates. Shaking limbs. Hands contracting into bird like claws. Faces contorted and twisted until too weak to even hold a tongue. The drooling. And towards the end only wasted shells lying limply on a sleeping mat. Those feeds ceased when it became clear there would be no survivors to interview. However, the fear and hopelessness could not be shut off. It spread faster than death.

Arnil was among the lucky, at the right time and place, and with a priority skill. She and her younglings boarded a transport and left Ruanae behind forever. Only then were they safe, rising above the planet and into the vacuum of space, leaving the invisible virus and the atmosphere that carried it.

Debarking on the orbital city, she, her colleagues and their broods made their way through the nervous corridors and into the Seed Ship. The clinicians spread out over the discs on which they were stationed, prepping cryo-pods not meant to be used for another five cycles, when it would begin its mission, taking select and trained Ruan to courageously venture into the unknown, to seed other planets and perpetuate their species. Instead, the pods were readied for the panicked and frightened islanders lucky enough to leave before the winds brought infection and death.

The *Anarokt* was designed as an act of hubris, a display of greatness and superiority. The Ruan were to reach out and seed a star. But on the planet of Ruanae there was no more hubris or greatness. A superior race was decimated by an unseen and unknown enemy, and the *Anarokt* was reduced to nothing more than a lifeboat.

Second Seed

A young officer finds himself in a difficult position as the remaining Seed Ship prepares to depart a dying world. Outside are all those who are not fortunate enough to gain a berth on the species' last chance at survival.

Laant watched the planet below, the blue of the wide oceans speckled with greens and browns of the many archipelagos. A gossamer veil of white clouds passed over the scene. He studied the southern hemisphere. Home. It looked peaceful from the bridge of the orbiting ship; an idyllic scene painted on the viewscreen. The warm blue waters brought back memories of morning swims, of sails with his older brother before being chosen. Those early times etched so strongly into the synapses of memory. He could not lose them even if he wanted. He should forget, he knew, but he kept the memories safe, like a prisoner with a hidden jewel that the guards would never find.

Soft sand between his toes. He was not supposed to crave pleasure. But soft sand between his toes, a warm sun on his naked flesh ... Laant breathed out a laugh, a mere snort of air from his nostrils that nobody noticed. He was the guard now. Guarding secret memories, guarding his people. What was left of them. Maybe if he was able to fully complete his training, he could purge such thoughts, such cravings or aversions. To be a Guardian was to be above the common concerns of the people. It was to be responsible for the people, for the continuance of culture, to guard against threats both external and internal. His training was cut short by circumstance, which meant he had to continue by training himself.

Laant knew that the planet below was only peaceful, or *idyllic*, from a distance. Part of the northern hemisphere lay in shadow. The islands below absorbed the darkness, becoming an inseparable part of the blackness. All the cities slept so deeply that no dawn would ever waken them. No light escaped the night that would soon spread over the entire world. Laant pursed his lips. There was no place for hyperbole in his thinking. Not anymore. He must practice precision of thought and action.

He closed his eyes and heard the panicked shouting, the desperate pleas, the gunfire that he so recently left below. He was meant to feel compassion for the people, to show only strength, to *be* only strength. They were supposed to feel secure in his presence. He was ashamed that he felt fear instead. He wanted to run as far away from them as he could. In the end they all did, those of his cohort that survived.

"Ensign!"

He was drifting, his mind wandering, and he was on duty. He could not afford distraction. Laant blinked and sat up in his chair. It took a moment for him to realise that the Controller was addressing him. He was not yet used to the new rank. Only recently he was a mere cadet. Promotions happened quickly these days. There were many vacancies to fill, many that would never be filled. The controller himself was new to the role, never meant to lead this ship. These ships were designed to seed the Ruan seed in the far stars. The Seed Ship *Anarokt* had already departed, not taking the chosen few to find and build a new world as originally designed, but evacuating refugees from a dying planet, the grand ship nothing but a lifeboat.

Laant looked at the other crew on the bridge, Guardians he just met. Were they hiding inner turmoil like himself? The astrogator, sitting in front of his terminal, avoiding eye contact as he finalised the course. The second controller, looking too young for the role he was thrust into, his chin firmly jutting outward in a false display of confidence. Systems specialists, checking life support and cryo-chamber efficacy. Communications with the five discs making up the body of the massive ship. The engineer, operating the reactors that would take the ship to another star, and another planet they could call home. Was the moistness from his eye emotion escaping down the side of his face?

He tried not to speculate too deeply on where the original crew were. Were they *merendt*? Laant corrected his thought, to show respect for the dead and dying in the northern hemisphere. They were all Ruan, like himself, and deserved his honour and service, wherever they may have originated. A *merendt* was an animal, domesticated to bring pleasure and comfort, kept in the houses of the northers, treated almost as Ruan. What else did they call their northern ken? *Fonnen*. Soft. Southers thought the northers soft. Domesticated, like their pets. They used the term derogatorily. Now, there were no longer northers or southers, there were only survivors. The disease that began in the north spread throughout the entire planet. None were safe where it touched. None survived the pandemic. Whoever it infected died. They could find no cure, no origin, no pattern. All that was certain was the death in its wake as it travelled in the winds that swirled and followed the great currents of the oceans.

Maybe the original crew were still alive, locked down in the Sky City. Laant had a momentary glimpse of what it might be like in the once glorious structure. He pushed the image out of his mind and repeated a mantra for those trapped inside, sealed remotely from the surface when the contagion arrived. All escape pods deactivated, all shuttles disabled, all docking bays sealed. Those on the city were no doubt trying to override the safety measure and escape without triggering fail safes. There had been no explosions from the complex, nor exiting craft. They may still be trying. Or they may all be dead.

Laant looked at the structure. Next to the ship he was in, it was considered the greatest triumph of Ruan technology. Except what he saw was an empty and dead shell. Once they leave, how long will it continue to orbit the dead planet below? He could do the mathematics. Laant enjoyed calculations. The life of the power cells, the absence of replenishment or maintenance, the speed and height of orbit. A quick assessment gave him a figure of four hundred to five hundred years before it fell into the atmosphere, a fiery comet that would be seen by none, finally disappearing beneath the waves. His people might leave ruins behind, for a time, at least, but not their greatest achievement.

"Ensign!" His mind was wandering again, seeking shelter from reality.

"Yes, Controller!" he responded.

"Identify that ship," the Controller said.

Laant passed a hand over the monitor in front of him and examined the readings. A ship had just left the atmosphere. He opened his hand and the image grew larger. He could faintly see the thrust of the approaching ship. He opened his hand again and it grew still larger. He computed its flight from a southern island and on a course directly towards their ship. As soon as his sensor targeted the ship, its identification beacon grew dark.

"It has ghosted, Controller," Laant reported.

"Establish contact, Ensign."

Laant opened radio contact. "You are approaching the Seed Ship *Knrarokt* on an unauthorised flight plan," he said. "Identify yourself and state your intention."

In response, the light from the ship's reactor increased.

"They are increasing thrust, Controller," Laant said without turning away from the monitor.

"Establish contact, Ensign," he responded. "Let them know what will happen if they do not respond."

Laant swallowed. "Unidentified ship, state your intention or we will be forced to fire upon you." He looked at the controller, who nodded and gestured at the monitor, an order to repeat the message.

"I repeat, we will be forced to fire upon you if you fail to reply."

"Now target weapons, Ensign," the controller said. "Ready the plasma canon."

Laant did as he was told. As soon as weapons were locked on the approaching target, their identification beacon flickered briefly, only to go dark and remain that way. He locked the plasma canon on the target once the weapon signalled its preparedness. The controller nodded, issuing a silent order that Laant understood. He raised his first finger in front of the computer monitor and bent the middle knuckle, making it point downward. The plasma canon shot a flash of molten light that crossed in front of it's nose cone.

The other ship's radio came to life, and Laant and all those on the bridge with him listened to a struggle playing out on the approaching ship. Muffled shouts, the crash of equipment, finally the report of a weapon, and a voice emerging from the sudden silence.

"*Knrarokt*! *Knrarokt*! Our identifying beacon is disabled. Please do not shoot! Guardian, we are secure in your presence!"

"Identify yourself, reduce acceleration, and alter your course," Laant said. His eyes went to the controller, who nodded approvingly.

"This is the transport freighter *Strade*. We have a cargo of two hundred passengers from the uninfected island of Ruboaen. We seek refuge, please, Guardian." The speaker was cut short by the sound of glass shattering. Another report from a weapon brought silence.

The light from the ship's reactor dimmed, but its course did not falter.

"What is happening, *Strade*?" Laant asked.

A voice different from the first responded. "We have subdued a disturbance on the bridge, but are now in control. We ask for refuge, Guardian. We are in need."

If asked for refuge, a Guardian was to provide it, even if it led to their death. This every Guardian was taught, from their first days as cadet. But the *Knrarokt* was sealed, as was the fate of all those left behind.

"We can offer no succour," the controller said, to himself, to Laant, to all those on the bridge.

"*Strade*, deviate your present course as requested," Laant said.

"We cannot do that," the voice said. "There is nowhere for us to go. We need your assistance! We seek refuge! Our arrival time is—"

"Deviate your present course as requested," Laant repeated. "We are a closed destination." The controller's face was stone, devoid of emotion. Laant tried to copy it, to bury his fear.

"We cannot do that!" the voice responded. "There is no place to deviate to! Please, do not let us die! We are broods, only broods, children, women. Please, Guardian, we seek refuge."

"There can be no refuge on the *Knrarokt*," the controller said, looking at his crew. "We can risk no infection. Our purity must remain unthreatened."

"*Strade*, alter your course immediately," Laant said, the pleading in his voice unmissable.

"My name is Treelek," the voice said. "I have a wife. Her name is Sunil. We have a brood of four younglings. They are all here. Please, help us."

"Ensign, eliminate this threat to the *Knrarokt*," the controller ordered.

"Please," Laant said, opening begging this time. "Alter your course!"

"Ensign!" the controller shouted.

"Guardian! My name is Treelek! I request refuge for myself and my brood, for all the broods on board, for—"

Please, Laant shouted in his mind. *Please deviate!* But the *Strade* did not alter its course, approaching what it thought was its last chance for safety. Laant watched as his hand moved of its own accord. It passed lightly over the monitor and took control of weapons.

"—the sake of us all! We are secure in your presence! We are—"

The index finger of Laant's hand twitched, activating the plasma canon. A molten slug shot across the vacuum. The *Strade* exploded in a flash of light. The bridge of the *Knrarokt* was as silent as the space outside. Laant could feel the liquid emotion escape his eyes and run freely down his cheeks.

"Return to your duties," the controller said, each word forced, each word prying the crew from the moment that held them.

"Engineer," he said, louder. "Prepare reactors for acceleration."

"Yes, Controller," the engineer answered. The engineer manipulated his hands over his monitor, beginning activation sequences in the massive reactors located over two kilometres away at the stern of the vessel. In between were the five discs, each half a kilometre in diameter, filled with equipment and supplies for building a new world, and thousands of Ruan suspended in cryogenic sleep, for a voyage designed to take centuries. Acceleration would increase until the ship eventually travelled at fourteen gravities, enough force to turn any Ruan outside of a cryo-pod into a liquid mess.

"Secure your stations and report to cryo-pods for acceleration," the controller said to the bridge crew.

"Ensign," he added. "Power down weapons."

"Yes, Controller," Laant heard himself answer.

One by one, bridge crew left their stations. Laant was among the last. He powered off his monitor, leaving ship's defenses to the AI that would be responsible for all of their lives as the ship crossed the great expanse. He stood and straightened his tunic. His eyes met the controller's, but they were unreadable. He could feel the gravity slowly increase as he lay in his cryo-pod. The ship was underway, leaving its orbit of their home world, the birthplace they would never see again. He felt a needle slide into his arm, and another probe between ribs until finding his liver. Chemicals were injected. He welcomed the darkness and oblivion that rushed upon him, felt comfort in the coldness spreading throughout his body, turning him into unfeeling ice.

There are no dreams in cryosleep, a small blessing. But the time taken to sink into the icy oblivion was enough. Laant knew dreams did not operate in linear time. A moment, no matter how brief, could contain a lifetime of image and story. As he felt his consciousness fade, he was also aware of others around him. His elder brother, guiding the small vessel across the waves, his eyes communicating joy and love. His mother sat nearby. That was not a true image. Despite being a youngling, he never remembered his mother joining them. And yet here she was. He smelled the sea, the freshly caught fish at the bottom of the boat, even the scent of his mother. That was how he knew, on some level, that he was dreaming. That awareness should have added control to his dreaming, but he was a helpless spectator, watching himself from someplace outside, and yet also from within. He looked at his hand, in this dream that felt so real. He watched as one finger was raised, his fore finger. He watched as he bent his finger at the knuckle. And he watched his brother and his mother burst into flames, the fire from their bodies spreading to the boat, running up the mast and sails, and covering his own body.

Laant wanted to scream, but no noise escaped his mouth. Instead, he sat in front of the Selector, in another dream, tasked with finding adept younglings to become future Guardians. The Selector held a prize in his palm, and it was Laant's task to grab and claim it. The Selector held the shiny bauble in his hand, palm up. Laant reached for it and had his grasping fingers slapped by the Selector's other hand. Laant tried again and received another slap. He tried to reach out quicker, only to receive a stronger slap. His fingers tingled and his hand throbbed. For the briefest of moments, or ages of eternity in the time measured in dreams, Laant the ensign sat before the Selector. Then, he was a mere youngling again, unaware that he would soon leave his brood and never see them again. He reached for the bauble, slowly this time, giggling, aware of the futility of trying. But this time the Selector did not strike. He held his open palm still and allowed Laant to take what he held. It was a finger. The Selector smiled.

Laant tried to feel warmth in the Selector's smile, but could only feel a creeping cold that originated from deep within, until nothing but darkness and ice remained.

A Little Night Action

They think. They feel. They want to live, just like us. Using the latest technology, activists (or some might argue, terrorists) fight for animals that aren't able to defend themselves ...

She lifted the hard plastic case out of the locker and set it on the table. Releasing the clips and opening the lid, she gazed at the contents.

"Where's David?" she asked without turning.

"He's still sick."

"How can somebody be sick for three days!" She grabbed the table as the boat swayed, leaned over to view down the hatch and saw David lying on a bench.

"Hey!" she shouted. "Are you in this or not?"

David turned a pale face and looked at her with glassy eyes. He slowly closed them and lay his head back down.

"Fuck!" she said. "Get over here, kid, you're David now."

The young man left the railing he was clutching and staggered to the table in the centre of the deck. He looked at her, waiting for instructions. He didn't know how to be David. David had recruited him for the trip, but he hardly knew David. It was his first action, so when asked to come, he accepted without having to think twice. New recruits could wait months, or more, before they were trusted to go out. As he watched her marvel at what was in the case, he realised he didn't even know her name. She turned it so he could see inside.

"Come closer," she said. "Touch it."

He wrinkled his nose.

"This is what it's all about, kid. It'll be a game changer." She spoke loudly and passionately in that way that both frightened and reassured him. "They'll think twice before sucking everything out of the ocean."

She looked at him, waiting for him to reach out. He hesitated.

"Oh, for fuck's sake," she said. "Can you smell anything? No? That means it's fresh." She laughed at a joke he didn't understand.

He reached out a finger and touched it, pressing against its flesh. He ran it down its side. Then he lifted his finger to his nose and smelled it.

"You're such a moron," she said.

"The scales look so real."

"The whole thing looks real," she said. "Watch this." She tapped a key on her laptop and an image filled the screen. The cabin came into focus, and in front of that, themselves.

"That's us!" he said. He turned and looked at the case, and then to the screen to see the back of his head.

"Perfect optics. That's how we find the net," she said. "Then the equivalent of a brick of C-4 ends their fucking fishing."

"That has what in it? You made me touch it!"

"Relax, newbie," she said. She squinted her eyes as she grinned. "It isn't activated yet. I'll do that when it's in their net. They won't know what hit them. They might cotton on after three or four ships catch our babies."

"I don't want to kill fish," he said. "I'm here to protect them."

"Is this your first time out?" she asked

"Yeah, David said—"

"Fuck me," she interrupted. "Listen. The fish in the net, they're already dead. They've been suffocated and crushed to death. It's bloody horrible. But you have to step up now that Sicko is incapacitated. Consider it a battlefield promotion.

We're here to stop the slaughter of thousands, of millions. Are you going to flake out now?"

"No," he said. "I want to stop it too."

"Good, so get ready."

She left him by the case and walked through the cabin to reach the wheelhouse. She studied the screens illuminating the room, making little sense of what she saw.

"How we doing, skipper?"

"Almost in range," he said.

"Great. That them there?" she asked, looking out the window and pointing at red and white lights rising and falling across the black water.

"That's them," the skipper said. "Red over white, fishing tonight. That's what those lights mean. Fuckers work around the clock, never give it a rest."

"Will they see us?"

"Yep. But I hacked the automatic identification system. According to their radar we're a charter out for a bit of night fishing," he said. "If you're going to do this, now's the time. I'll keep us local."

She returned to the case. The young man stood beside it just as she left him, not sure what to do with his hands or the rest of his body. She shook her head and typed in the activation code on her laptop. The eyes inside the case lit red. Waving the young man over, she indicated for him to pick it up. He took it in both hands, bumping the table with his hip as the swell lifted the boat.

"Watch it, for fuck's sake," she hissed. "Now put it in the harness."

He followed her finger to a length of line tied to straps made of rubber, carried it over and carefully inserted it. Now that it was out of the case, he could see it was mechanical. Its body was narrow and silver, with a dorsal fin rising out of its back, and the tell-tell dark markings on its rounded head just like a silver warehou. But its red, illuminated eyes and jointed tail were definitely not natural.

She bent over her laptop. "Now lower it over," she said, but he didn't hear.

He waited, watching her. For somebody so small, she exuded a great deal of strength, he thought. If she weren't so scary, he might have been attracted to her.

"New David!" she called. Not hearing a response, she turned and faced him. "Okay, so what is your name, then?'

"Cody," he said.

"Of course, it is," she said. "Cody, raise the antenna in the dorsal fin and lower the goddamned fish over the side. And be careful!"

He noticed the small wire in the fin, pinched it and pulled. It withdrew from the fish for thirty centimetres before stopping. Then he raised the fish over the railing and reached out over the water as he lowered the harness. When it was fully submerged, the mechanical fish squirmed as if testing its muscles before darting out and disappearing into the dark sea. Cody joined her at the laptop, peering at the screen.

"It's dark," he said.

"Of course, it is," she said. "It's under the water, and its night time." She tabbed a key and adjusted the fish's course. "Watch this," she added. "Thermal imaging."

She pressed another key and the dark on the screen turned a hazy navy blue. After several minutes a yellow and orange glow appeared. She guided the fish over the top of the mass before taking it around the other side.

"Butchers!" she spat. "Look at all of them."

She guided the fish back over the haul until reaching the gapping mouth of the trawl net. Turning it around she let it be swallowed. The yellow and orange glow grew larger until it surrounded the fish. She typed commands on the laptop and it squirmed itself deep into the mass of the dead and dying.

Tears ran down her cheeks. "So many," she said. "So many ..."

Cody watched her as she stood in front of the screen, not knowing what to do or say, gingerly holding himself away, as if she had the equivalent of a brick of C-4 hidden somewhere inside her.

"What do we do now?" he asked carefully.

"Wait," she said, wiping her eyes with the back of her hand, sniffing, and wiping snot away with her palm. "We wait until they haul."

They stood over the laptop as minutes turned into an hour. Finally, motion sensors on the fish showed it was rising. She switched the image to visual and the dark on the screen turned to dim light. Then the light increased and they saw all the fish around theirs, and the view tumbled as it fell into the waiting pound below, the tank holding the catch until it was beheaded, sliced, gutted, weighed and frozen with others into solid blocks to then be shipped around the world to be fried, grilled, broiled or barbequed, and finally eaten. She felt the blood rush to her cheeks as she thought about it. She typed a code into her laptop, and stood up straight. Her eyes were now dry and her mouth set in a fierce frown as she pressed the tab key.

A large flash lit the night before the sound of the explosion reached them. They turned and watched the trawler burning across the water. The radio in the wheelhouse crackled.

"Mayday! Mayday! Mayday!" it screamed at them until the skipper turned the volume down. "Mayday! This is the fishing vessel *Armitage*. We are in need of immediate assistance. *Romeo! Romeo!* Please render assistance."

The three stared at the radio. David raised his head weakly and watched it with them. They flinched as it barked again.

"*Romeo! Romeo!* Please respond!" it called. "This is the fishing vessel, *Armitage*. We are in need of—" The skipper turned the radio off.

"Who's *Romeo*?" the woman asked.

"We are," the skipper said. "At least on their radar." He opened the throttle and the boat lurched forward and sped away from the scene.

"Nice," she said, grabbing hold of a bench to steady herself. "Romeo, oh Romeo, wherefore art thou, Romeo?"

Twisted Love

Can love survive not only difference, but the distance of time as well? Is it necessary to survive, or is it enough simply to connect in the time we have?

He touched his ear to turn off the translator device nestled there. Her voice was like operatic bird song, like wind through tall aspen, like—she playfully hit his hand and he lowered it.

"You're not even listening," she chastised, but there was no anger or disappointment in her tone, only amusement.

"I was listening," he protested. "You have the most beautiful voice."

She felt a softening warmth in the centre of her chest in reflection to the smile he wore. His blue eyes were so open and inviting. Her hand stroked his arm. She knew he saw the same invitation in her eyes.

"You asked me about our transmitter, but I intuit you were wanting more understanding," she said.

He ran his fingers through blue grass, letting the soft blades tickle his fingers. Their technology appeared to be purpose driven, unlike on Earth, where advances were made and exploited not because they were needed, but simply because they could. Or made to exploit resources under the ground or sea or deep in space. And worse, developed in times of war as ways to kill each other more efficiently. There was a lot he didn't want to tell her, that she didn't need to know, about how his own species used their inventiveness.

She could feel him hold back, but knew that his intention was right. Perhaps, she admitted to herself, there were things she didn't want or need to know. What he brought to her was wonderful. What was, right now, sitting beside her was giving freely of himself, if not needless details from his home. She felt the attraction as soon as she saw him, a glow among the small party that emerged from their ship. She touched him with her emotion and he glanced up, catching her eye, and he smiled.

"You call out to the stars, but don't try to go there," he said.

"The stars are here, every night, so why rush to them?" she teased. "Besides, they are so very far away, and there are more pressing things to do here."

"Like?"

"Like becoming, growing, expressing," she said. "Like loving. Isn't loving worth more energy than leaving?"

The way he bent his neck and turned to look—relaxed, smooth, tender. She felt the warmth in her heart descend lower.

"It is worth the energy," he said. "Loving."

"But you expended the effort," she admitted. "And I am glad. We sent an invitation, and you answered. I am grateful. And pleased you came so quickly."

"We came after four thousand years!"

"No," she said. "You twisted time and space and came as soon as we called! Isn't that what your captain said?"

"Corkscrewed," he corrected. "He said we corkscrewed time."

"That word is too odd," she said. "I prefer twisting. It is like limbs wrapping themselves around each other in love making." She wriggled closer to him and put her leg over his, sliding her foot beneath his calf. She sensed a moment of hesitation within him with the closeness, which faded like smoke. He reached an arm around her and pulled her close as they lay on the hillside.

"We twisted time and space," he conceded, "so that I could meet you and hold you and smell you!" He buried his nose in her thick green hair and inhaled deeply. Then he released her and lay on his back beside her, gazing up at the giant planet the moon orbited.

"Tell me how you did, how you came so quickly to me," she said, knowing he could not.

"I'm not a physicist!" he said. "I just study the air. The atmosphere."

"Same-same," she said. "Things you cannot see."

"Not same-same. One takes far more brains. It's not my field."

"You have a beautiful and caring brain," she said, leaning on an elbow and stroking his soil-coloured hair. Even his plain colours were beautiful. Eyes the colour of sky, hair the colour of soil, skin with so little colour she could trace the veins beneath.

"Folding I understand." She separated her thumb and middle finger. "A and B. Put A and B together, fold space, and travel like that." She brought her fingers together and snapped them.

He copied the motion, snapping his. "Just like that," he agreed. "There is a ship there now. Here, now. Then. Or will be."

"Now you are not making sense," she said.

"Four thousand years from now a ship will visit, in response to your call. To see who is still here. My ship was tasked with responding to the first call, to see who sent the original message. You," he said.

He knew their words were mere surface play, foreplay, but necessary. He felt a calmness in her presence that he lacked elsewhere in his life. Ambition, drive, desire to go or to be, all dropped away. Simply being near her caused a calm and inner warmth that told him everything was as it should be, that there was no place else to be, except right here and right now and right next to her. He turned and faced her. She was so beautiful that she glowed! She glowed ever since he felt her touch his mind, and he looked up and saw her among the welcoming group. Now he fell into her large emerald eyes.

"Your time," she said, bringing him back to a hillside covered in blue grass, overlooking a slow moving river, and farther in the distance, a radio transmitting station and a space ship.

"My time?" he asked.

"Four thousand years from now," she said. "When you were born. What does that make me, your grandmother?"

He sighed when she smiled. "A lot more than that," he said, trying to focus. "Right now, at this time on my planet people are building temples out of stone and using crude metal tools. They are ploughing the ground with wood and bones, learning how to cultivate crops. It's all just terrible timing. When you called, we couldn't listen, and your message travelled four thousand lightyears, so even if we could—"

"And as soon as you could you not only folded space, but you twisted time to see me," she said.

"Twisted it as hard as I could, to see you," he agreed. He stroked her cheek with his fingertips. Her skin was smooth and the colour of … sherbet, he decided, like the ice cream he enjoyed as a child. Such an amazing being! His chest swelled with gratitude that he was chosen for the response ship rather than concurrent contact. God only knows what that crew will find. Response was often merely a fly by, a record of what was; the secondary mission. Each time radio waves were detected that indicated sentient life through purposeful transmission, two ships were sent to investigate. Response was not meant to contact. But here they felt the attraction, each member of the crew, and they landed, and were greeted, and now here he was!

"I am so glad to be here," he said without thinking. "Here, with you. You are so beautiful. You make me feel …"

"Like there is peace in the universe," she finished. "Like there is no other place to be. Like you spent your life as half of a person, and now you have found the other half."

"Yes," he agreed.

She placed her hand on top of his, a gentle invitation. He turned his over and held hers, an acceptance. Her smile grew.

"Come," she said.

And they stood and she guided him down a neatly groomed path to the bottom of the hill where a tidy row of small houses stood. She led him up the front stairs to her home, and only released his hand once they were inside. She placed a hand on each of his shoulders and looked up into his eyes, and his hands found her hips. Their bodies vibrated with anticipation.

"Let us join," she said softly, and he followed her to the bedroom.

They undressed slowly in front of each other, both smiling, both mesmerised. She touched his bare chest, the dark hairs that covered his strong muscles. Such an exquisite creature, she thought in wonder. Her hand passed over his stomach, firmly rounded his hip until wrapping itself around his member. She could feel his body tremble. He gently cupped her breast, lifting it, bending and kissing her nipple, tasting it with his tongue. His other hand ran down her back, until it reached her bottom. She felt his energy increase, felt his urge to lose control.

He would need guidance. She stepped slightly back. "Lie down," she instructed.

He obeyed, lying on the bed. She stepped over him, lowering herself. Reaching between her legs, she moistened her fingers and rubbed them on the tip of his cock. Then she slowly lowered herself, guiding him into her, agonisingly slowly. When he tried to raise up to meet her, she pressed him down, controlling the penetration. When he was deep inside her, she sat motionless, straddling his hips, gripping his waist tightly with her thighs.

"Look at me," she said, and his eyes travelled up her belly and her breasts and her neck and met her gaze. "Stay with the energy, our energy," she said.

She started to massage him from within, a gentle pulsing that urged him to explode, but each time he reached the precipice, she slowed herself and held him as close to the edge as he could bear, increasingly building the energy between them. She breathed deeply in through her nose and exhaled slowly from her mouth, in rhythm with her vagina, and soon he breathed with her, until they became one breath, one energy, one light, one being. After what felt like a moment, or an hour, or an eternity, she placed a hand on the middle of his chest and closed her eyes and he knew it was permission to climax.

They lay together in her bed as the day began to fade. Soft light filtered through the window. His mind began to wonder, to fantasise about bringing her home, how lonely she might feel, how alien. He dreamed of staying with her, on this world, the only member of his species. Could he fit in? Could he leave everything behind? He gazed at her resting face. Her eyes were closed and she breathed softly. He knew she wasn't asleep. Maybe she was thinking similar thoughts. Maybe she, too, wanted to just push them aside, to be in this moment, this wonderful moment. He closed his eyes and surrendered to what he knew as the only truth.

Bunk Mate

Space can be a lonely place. Distances are measured in months, not miles. In the early days of NASA, they thought the vast emptiness and solitude would be too much for the human mind to handle. Maybe they were right ...

He's up there wanking. I know that sound. Slap slap slap slap. For fuck's sake. And I have to be awake, staring at the bottom of his bunk. At least it isn't moving. I could hit the bunk, make a loud noise to say, knock it off, I'm right below you! But that would make for an awkward work day tomorrow. Catching a guy wanking. Not a good thing to let him know that you know. Ever watch a dog crap, the look on its face? That's what he looks like when he gets caught, or finds out you caught him. I'll pick up this tablet and swipe instead, distract me from his slap slap slap slaping. It doesn't even sound like he's trying to be quiet, but he probably thinks he is. And how can he wank on his back? I've never managed that. Okay, so 'never' is an exaggeration. It's just not easy.

Maybe the gravity from acceleration is helping, extra weight to stay horizontal. I just put deep heat all over my hands because every fucking muscle seems to hurt. Tendons, ligaments, whatever the hell holds my fingers together. It's not that carpal tunnel crap, they're just sore from hard work. I have trouble imagining it. Doing the same thing so many times that you damage your hands? Try doing something else, for fuck's sake. He's probably going to give himself carpal tunnel the way he's slapping. Finish, already! But God, don't let me hear *that*. I'm already going to hear slapping the next time he talks to me. I don't think I could handle the finishing overture. Now deep heat on hands is a sure way to keep your hands off yourself. I learned on these deep long hauls you need distractions, and wanking just turns into addiction. It feels good, and makes that brain chemical, serotonin or something, a happy hormone if I remember that right—I probably don't, but I don't care what it's called. It's why there's no porno on this ship, unless he secreted some on. It's way too easy to leave the maintenance and watch a babe get fucked all ways from Sunday. Oral, followed by fingering followed by tonguing followed by cowgirl reverse cowgirl doggy missionary and finally the money shot. Yeah, that's the picture. Push it out of mind now because deep heat on a cock burns too much and is hard to wash off and I ain't going to wank because the son of a bitch above me is wanking. Because that would be the reason why I was doing it and I don't want to go there. This seems to have worked. It's quiet up top, small mercies. Now to think of something else so I quit thinking about tits and ass on porn I don't have. I don't know, dead fish, auntie's apple pie, the job list for tomorrow. There's always that, and a lot of tomorrows until docking. Jobs list. Yeah, that did it. Good enough anyway. Turn this device off and daydream fantasise to sleep. Dream porn.

*

His bunk looks unslept in, like it was made by a recruit in basic training. The sheet. four fingers wide, folded crisply over the blanket, all tucked firmly under the mattress so you'd practically need a crowbar to pry them apart to get in. What's that saying? Tight enough to bounce a quarter on? Whatever a quarter is. The bed looks like it did when we first boarded. I'm surprised they don't come wrapped in plastic. Just made up real tight. What does that say about the guy, making his bed that way every day? Anal retentive? Psychotic? Obsessive compulsive? What's that acronym? OCD? I'll have to watch how many times he touches the door handle before using it, or whatever weird habits he has. Might be a fun distraction, a bit of zoology, studying the primate in his not so natural surroundings. He's not here, of course, up early and down in the cargo hold or some outer corridor. Ships the size of … I don't know, what kind of clever analogy can I use? Ships the size of space freighters. It takes at least an hour to walk from one end to the other in this kind of g. That's big, meaning lots of space, and all the company allocates to the human on maintenance and the computer running the damn ship is one cabin and one bridge and one tiny galley. The bridge is smaller than the cabin. The galley is smaller than the bridge. The rest of the space is for the cargo. Get the general design? I guess the cargo's where the money is, after all, not making it comfortable for me. I'm just the guy who has to live on the damn thing for months as it transits the solar system. I'm just the guy making sure nothing breaks, keeping the door knobs polished, checking the reactor, blah blah blah. Listen to me bitch. What's the mantra? Count the money. Every day adds up to a fat pay check at the other side. Speaking of which, there's a panel half off in corridor 3b on second level hiding a half finished recircuit that needs finishing.

*

I must have fallen asleep before he came in, and woke too late to catch him. Catch him? Why would I want to do that? I'd rather not hear anything again. Oh yeah, his coffee. He has a stash somewhere. I can smell when he makes it, that scent wafting from the galley and I float towards it like a wolf in a cartoon being dragged by the nose towards a pretty lady. I didn't bring porn, but I brought a collection of ancient cartoons. They crack me up. I understand that saying now. My ribs actually hurt form laughing. Like I cracked them. Get it? The cartoon ladies have of late started to look too sexy, so I hid them away. Only problem is, I know where I hid them. His coffee is another story. By the time I reach the galley, he and his coffee are gone. Time for a proper look.

*

I took the galley apart. Literally. I unpacked all the stores. I checked all the cupboards. I searched under any spaces that had an under. I took off the fridge door and even looked inside it. The door. It's just tightly packed foam, if you're wondering. Not a bag, not a cafetière, not even a fucking single ground of coffee. Once everything was put back in place, I took it apart again, checking inside any stores that were opened, opening those that might be big enough to hide some beans. Maybe that's what he's done, spread out the beans into little individual sized bags, as small as a tea bag. Or stashed each precious bean at the bottom of every bag or box or can. The cans are still bothering me. They're sealed shut, you can't open one and close it again with a coffee bean inside and make it look like it's never been opened! Can you? I'm starting to think the coffee isn't in the galley.

*

I'm starting to think this bunk mate is fucking with me, or I'm going mad. I don't like shipping with others. Two doesn't work out here. Never does. You end up driving each other crazy, or killing each other. Or worse. I don't even remember boarding with the fuck. I'll keep some notes on this tablet so there's some bread crumbs to the truth at least. Find out what his game is and stop it. I found a panel half off in corridor 3b on second level hiding a half finished recircuit job. That shit isn't rocket science, just tedious as hell, and not something that should be left half done. I took out a driver and magged it to the bulkhead, removed the panel, and reached for my tool. Nothing but empty wall. Okay, a mental lapse. I was sure I stuck it on the wall like I always do. Lose a driver once and you become, what's the term? OCD about them. Remove your tool, mag it to a wall, prepare the work, then access the tool. It's not obsessive, it's being organised, and they don't go missing. But when I reach up, nothing but wall. I looked in my tool pouch and there's no driver. I empty the pouch, even shake out a piece of lint from the bottom. Okay, I think, so he's pulling a fast one, trying to wind me up. I think I'm clever and I can catch the fuck. I accessed the lights to stop them automatically turning on as I approached, stood up and quietly walked down the corridor. At the corner to 3c I stopped, and looked around the bend and couldn't see a thing. It was too fucking dark. Okay, so I'm not so clever. Fuck him. I went back to the panel and reactivated the lights, walked to 3c and, yes, it was empty. Big fucking surprise. Where's my fucking driver?

*

A conversation. I can write down the random conversations we have. That ought to keep me distracted. Always have something to occupy the mind. That's what they say, anyway, company HR desk pilots pretending to be psyches or weathered spacers. Dumb term that—there's no weather in space. Do a few hauls and you look it, though. He looks it. He always has stubble on his face that's like a five-day beard. And tired eyes with those bags underneath. "Not to be too personal," he says, "but I can't hold much pee. I had my prostrate out six years ago. The big C. Cancer. But they caught it early or I'd be dead. I had a bag for a while, but I was lucky." Yeah, not to be too personal. I made him a cup of coffee. My stash will never make the whole trip, but he needs it, and I feel like a dick sometimes drinking on my own, which defeats the whole purpose. I'm supposed to enjoy it. "I just had a big birthday coming up, you know, one with a zero in it, so I asked the doctor to check. Guys are way too shy about letting their doctor stick a finger up their ass. That guy's finger saved my life. Not that I'd wish what came after on anybody else. Chemo wreaks havoc on your body. And surgery. I didn't think I'd be able to get hard again, ever. That's a scary thought when you have to face it. I had to wear those pads too. Whatever you call them, they're still just diapers for grown-ups. My partner couldn't handle it all so found somebody else to fuck. How's that for a punch in the guts, to follow a punch in the crotch? But it came back, thank God. My hard on. A lot of the times it doesn't, for other guys, I mean. Mine's working fine now. I got a lady Earth side that puts up with me not being there most of the time. She makes it work just fine." Not-to-be-too-personal. Mental note, do not participate in conversations that start with that phrase. I can't remember any more of it. I think my mind rebelled, found it all too much, and just went someplace else. It happens in traumatic events. The mind just erases it, or hides it somewhere safe. One minute he's being too personal, the next I'm at the small table in the galley with two mugs of coffee in front of me, both cold. I looked in the cabin, but it was empty.

*

I hate drift. With thrust, things stay down. Like internal organs. In drift I can't feel my bladder, so I wake up every hour because I either need to go or I'm just too worried about wetting the bed. I can't bring myself to wear those goddammed diapers. There's still a carton on the bunk above that I refuse to open. So, I unstrap from my cot, float to the lav, stick my limp cock in the suction tube and watch a drop or two run out. I should take the mirror out of that room. God, I look tired. When did my eyes gets those bags? This haul is really taking it out of me. I can keep a pee diary on this tablet, make a spread sheet, times, amounts, colours, last intake of fluids. Sounds like a fruitful project. A worthwhile distraction, as HR would say. Or, there's a panel half off in corridor 3b on second level hiding a half finished recircuit that needs finishing. I'm already up, so I might as well finish it.

About the stories

I wrote *The Ethnographer's Gift* quite a few years ago. It sat in a folder, a real one, probably manila, and gathered dust. And then for some reason I took it out. I had just started a PhD and was writing a lot. It was academic writing, so maybe I craved the creative. I let a friend from China read it and valued his feedback. He gave straight forward and honest appraisal, pointing out parts that may not have made sense or caused a little confusion. So, I drafted, or started to practice that process. A story is seldom, if ever, written down once and finished. I spent another couple of years letting it sit in a folder, this time electric, tweaked it a bit more and finally sent it away for publication. Much as I found academic writing constraining, it did force writing and editing skills to improve, and there was plenty of feedback built into the process to encourage that.

The idea of death moments comes from the Buddhist idea of the death mind—the mind we take into death and into our next incarnation. Do we leave this life full of fear? Regret? Anger? Can we cultivate our mind while living to exit this life with a calm and loving and accepting mind? It must be rare, indeed, to exit that way, the way Chloe did. But it is how I would like to leave—not in front of a taxi on a busy street, but with a calm acceptance, to be able to observe, 'oh, this is my death moment.' That can sound a little morbid, but if you're walking around with that kind peace and acceptance, you're life moments will be even richer.

Earth Story is an idea that I had as a young boy. Well, kind of. I looked at our civilization and wondered if anything would be left after millions of years, if any evidence of our 'greatness' might survive. Probably not, right? Which started me wondering about what evidence of others had been scrubbed clean by time during the past millions of years. There was a time when the prehistoric creatures roaming this amazing planet weren't so ferocious, before those scary dinosaurs with teeth and claws evolved. What kind of place might that have been, and who might have lived here at that time? A lot of contact between life forms is probably accidental that way. We have only been here for such a short time, which is really a very narrow window to happen to have an alien species fly by. We might not only need to travel over distances, but also through time. But that is for another story.

And speaking of aliens flying by, *Journey to the Stars* looks in that dark corner of our minds that think it's all a bit kind of scary. I mean, a lot of 'true life' encounters involve things like nasty probes, so who's to say we can trust those aliens? An original version of this story was written in a pub in England almost twenty years ago. It was neat finding an old copy and seeing how my writing has improved. Or rather, how bad my writing was back then. That first copy was sent to a magazine, back when you physically put them in an envelope and used a stamp. The magazine had three people read it, probably graduate students at a university somewhere vetting stories for free, er, I mean, for the work experience. If a submission got three ticks of approval from the readers, then it progressed towards publication. Two of the readers really liked the story. The third left a comment saying something about me being sick in the head.

With *The Locker Room* I wanted to write something based very closely on lived experience, to take an experience and turn it into a story. I wasn't a marine, or involved in a war in space— but I worked on a deep-sea trawler for four weeks with the characters in the story. The locker room on the ship was where we kitted up before we went into the factory once the net was hauled. Coveralls, hairnets, steel toed gum boots, gloves. That was our armour, and the shift was close enough to combat.

The locker room was a special place, a place in between, where we spent the few moments we had sharing, or ribbing, or griping. I kept a journal during that trip, writing in it when I had any energy or free time (which wasn't very often!) What I didn't write down I committed to memory. Sure, I took a writer's liberty in changing the setting, and some of the dialogue, but most of what our soldiers say was close to that on the factory ship. I warned them that they'd end up in a story, as a platoon on a spaceship. I dedicated this book to them. I found that I was making mental notes, as well as scribbles in the margins of my notebook, on character traits and some of their quirks, as well as what I was going through.

What I also wanted to explore was leaving a lot of questions unanswered in the small space of the short story, but not so many that I'd lose the reader, or the theme of the story itself. I was warned by a content editor I worked with on my first novel to be careful with 'riddling'. We can be tempted as writers to leave questions, to let the reader work things out for themselves, or to set up future reveals. But it can be a delicate balance. *The Locker Room* let me play with this, to experiment with essential information, what the reader needed to know, and what they didn't really need to know. Who were these characters fighting? When did this war take place? Where were they? Who was the narrator? What was his story? We just don't know—all we know is what he told us. I enjoyed that about being in a situation like the trawler, as our narrator says at the end of the story. All my co-workers knew about me was what I decided to share. And that was enough for them, as well as for the story. It was just a snapshot, just a scene, in a space in between their story, where we drop in and visit these soldiers before they make a drop into combat.

I am humbled by that powerful thought: we *all* have a story. All of us! It changes the way I see people, and inspires me to try to write story better. That's the joy of not just writing, but the process of growth that comes through writing and writing and writing, and working with others that know their craft.

Landing Party is, admittedly, a tad Twilight Zone-ish. The seed of the idea actually comes from a scene in Robert A. Heinlein's *Glory Road*. The characters are working their way through somewhere, and then things close in, and they have to crawl. But the only one who sees things close in is the hero the others are following. It was all in his head. They didn't know why he was crawling, but he was leading, so they crawled as well. He thought what he was seeing was real, but it was planted in his consciousness by who or what was trying to stop him. That's the idea that stuck with me since reading that book as a teenager. *The Matrix*! You might think. Reality is not what we think it is! I wonder if the makers of that movie read *Glory Road*. It's an old idea, older than the Buddha. There is also a story by Ray Bradbury, one of my favourites, about explorers landing on a new world, and being overcome with the strongest desire to just return to Earth. No matter what, they just have to get home. What they can't see, what they are prevented from seeing, is that they are all covered in alien spores. Great stuff.

This group of explorers see something else, and whatever inhabits that planet wants something different. Rather than the barren rock they saw above, they find soft and inviting moss, just right for laying down, and, well … Here I try to use an idea that crops up in *Twisted Love*, the use of sexual energy in Tantric Buddhism. Sex, in Tantra, is using the energy created through arousal. That energy is meant to be developed and channelled throughout the entire body (not squandered in ejaculation). Only, rather than increase the vitality of out landing party, it seems that something is feeding off it.

I wrote an earlier version of this story quite a while ago that involved a teenager finding a cave, and showing it to his friends. They enter and find a wonderland. Lush vegetation, a river, fruit, that kind of thing. They stay and explore it and enjoy it, and, yep, are never seen again. The protagonist gets a brief glimpse of being surrounded by the bones of any creature that ever wandered inside.

But I was encouraged to scribble this story after a dream. Quite a few stories come from dreams. Maybe it's where the imagination has fewer self-imposed constraints. The *Lucid* series all started that way—an actual lucid dream, where I had to find a car and was struck by the thought, "what do I need a car for, I'm in a dream?" The night before I wrote *Landing Party,* I dreamed about a strange hamlet I walked through. Looking into a small house, I might see a woman in bed, so I go in and to the bed and we make love, just like that, building and exploring sexual energy. And others would come and go, and for some reason it was all perfectly natural. And yet, there was something else, something a little not right in the hamlet, but I couldn't quite focus enough to see it. Or I didn't want to, because I was delightfully preoccupied.

QMS, like *The Locker Room*, comes from my work in fisheries. As the narrator explains, the acronym stands for Quota Management System. It's how we decide how much fish can be harvested form each area. New Zealand takes it very seriously—not just the government, but the industry itself. This story came out of my initial training to be a fisheries observer. Observers are government employees who go along on the fishing trip, as independent eyes, to assess the catches and conduct biological work on the fish species. Most deep-sea vessels are required to carry an observer during their weeks out at sea.

Just what might the future look like once those resources around the world start to get scarce? *QMS* is a novel in the works. The short story, written in the first person, stands alone, but also asks so much more. Being out at sea for weeks on end as an observer, there'll be a lot of opportunity to add chapters. But will a first-person voice work? Can a story ranging over the high seas be told from one person's perspective? I suppose *Moby Dick* was, but Ishmael stayed on one ship the whole time, and I want to range farther. In novel form, *QMS* will be told in the third person, which lets me present multiple points of view.

The primary characters will be Rickets, and also (yes, you guessed it) the fisheries observer, Moss. My first trip out allowed me to write a whole quarter of the novel, and brought some welcome fun and imagining into the routine of days in the factory. I get to research first hand. Like being on the bridge and asking the first mate what the names of various controls and winches are, as well as how to release the net in a hurry. I got to view Auckland Island, one of our sub-Antarctic possessions and a wildlife and marine reserve, through binoculars one sunny afternoon and decided to go there for a while in the story. Unfortunately, that research will be by book and search engine as fishing vessels can't stop and look around. *QMS* will be my first truly New Zealand based novel.

The story, *Solo*, stands alone, but it has parents (or maybe they're step-sisters). My first three published novels play with the theme of lucid dreaming—of being 'awake' in a dream, being conscious that you are the dreamer. In these books, *American Dreamer, Tomorrow's History*, and *Gods and Dreamers*, the dreamers find themselves in another reality, another time, expected to do something to affect the outcome of history. They are not acting alone, but at the behest or manipulation of a higher energy form, an energy fueled by people's beliefs or fears or adulation. We call these energy forms 'gods' or 'angles' or 'demons'. Some dreamers act for the gods, while some resist them. Call them Devotees and Resistors, at least until I come up with better names.

Now, taking this idea a little further, if we can dream lucidly and change history, by say, killing a baby that would grow up to be a future leader, or stopping that baby from dying, what if there was a particularly sick type of individual that just liked to kill? They could do so with impunity, while they slept. They could lucidly dream into another time, select their victim, and wake from that reality. That is the origin thought of *Solo*. Maybe that's why some serial killers never get caught— because they are no longer in our reality. I call these dreamers, Solos. There may be a fourth novel in the *Lucid* series, with *Solo* as its seed. But that would be a dark place to travel while writing and researching it.

The title, *Failure to Communicate*, comes from one of my favourite films, *Cool Hand Luke,* though the story is nothing like the movie. "What we have here," the warden says, "is failure to communicate." If you haven't seen it, then remedy that situation as fast as you can. Paul Newman at his coolest (he was always cool). And that's where anything involving that film stops. Three words from a phrase I liked. I sometimes murmur it quietly in an argument or when I'm on the phone with a bureaucrat at Maritime New Zealand.

The theme of *Failure to Communicate* is straight forward. We can't even communicate with dolphins, an intelligent mammal from on our own planet. How on earth (or off it) could we talk to alien life? This short story explores what might happen when we try. As a writer I wanted to practice using dialogue as a way to progress a story. That is much of the scene where Easton is speaking to her team. That entire section is told through dialogue, with a few beats to help the flow. I read in several advice books on writing to read dialogue aloud to help with authenticity, and I did that with this section, playing out the meeting Easton holds with her team, reading it aloud at my desk.

Where my drafts really changed was not in dialogue though, but imagery. The scene where Easton touches the Visitors first involved a more physical craft, but after letting it sit for some time, and listening to that inner voice that said something wasn't quite right, it turned into something more esoteric, which was, as with *The Locker Room*, based on personal experience. Not visiting a spaceship, but a type of dissolution experienced through meditation, briefly touching something that was beyond words or concepts.

Stepping Out, The Originals, and *Second Seed* all come from the MisStep universe. *MisStep* is my first science fiction novel (it's as yet unpublished.

I've sent it away for consideration). *Stepping Out* was written as a type of prologue for that story, set a few generations before. It builds the world that the characters in *MisStep* inhabit. The story stands alone quite nicely. It is one of my first experiments in form—an imaginary introduction replete with footnotes, and a journal without dates. There is a term, 'info drop', which can sometimes describe part of a story. It's where the author quite literally drops a lot information, which more often than not, should have been given to the reader in more subtle or clever ways. I dropped a lot of info in the footnotes, trying to get away with it that way. I figured that with that information in hand, you'd slip right into the world of *MisStep* and its main character, Andrew Jensen, which takes place about sixty years after *Stepping Out*.

Stepping Out has been selected for publication in the anthology, *Revolutions*, containing stories of social change and upheaval in future earths.

A 'reader magnet' is a piece of writing—a short story or collection of stories (like this one), a novella, even a novel—written for the purpose of attracting readers to your website and mailing list. Mailing lists are developed so that writers can communicate with their readers, and potential buyers of their books. Have you joined my mailing list? A magnet is developed to give a reader an incentive to sign up. It is a freebee—join the list and receive a free story/novella/novel. Marketing is a real learning curve! *Stepping Out* could act as reader magnet. But *Maritime Report* was developed with magnets in mind, even though I never used it for that. The first mate of the scow, Andrew Jensen, flees the planet, takes the first job on an interstellar freighter he can, and the novel *MisStep* begins. But nowhere in *MisStep* is an adequate explanation of what exactly happened on Earth, and why he had to flee so quickly—it just sits in the back of the story. The main character has nightmares, flashes of the evening he killed his skipper, but he never talks about it. In the follow up novel *Seeders*, more is revealed, including what strings Jens pulled to get that job in space.

To be honest, I enjoyed writing the death of his skipper. It was healing, in a way. I got to rid myself of a bully in real life in one of the ways a writer can. A writer can kill with impunity, stick a knife in their ribs, throw them overboard, and get away with it. Even feel a hell of lot better after doing it.

I may have said earlier that *Stepping Out* was some of my first experimenting with form, but I think *Maritime Report* may have actually been the first. I just finished studying and qualifying for my inshore skipper license and thought I'd have a go at writing my own incident report.

Benthic material, as you know by now, is whatever is found in nets once they are hauled. Typically, these nets have been used on the ocean floor, called bottom trawling. Depending on where you are fishing, there might be a lot of material, or hardly any. Some areas are so well fished, not much comes up. The odd piece of rope, a piece of sponge, a rock. Other places might contain lots of garbage, from the days when anything got chucked over the side of a boat. Some places are off limits, because the ocean floor needs protecting. Fishery Observers keep an eye out for anything benthic, especially vulnerable species of coral. And little visitors from other planets, of course.

The table in the story *Benthic Material* is at a pub in Nelson called The Ale House, and we drank a few too many pints with a tutor one evening. The story wasn't his, he didn't even talk about stuff from the sea floor, but those on my training course are there, at least some of them. Zak and Rachel and Tree all trained to be observers with me. This story was one of those that just popped into my mind, and then flowed right onto paper. It makes up part of the collection of deep-sea influenced stories.

Close Encounter is a type of writing called 'flash fiction', or 'micro story', that plays with contact and communication like *Failure to Communicate*. Flash fiction is often limited to five hundred words. I managed five hundred and forty with this one. Part of my work is recording sea birds and interaction with the vessel out on the ocean, and watching the big beautiful albatross fly over and around gave birth to the idea that maybe they're not always alone up there. Maybe we're not, for that matter, but we just can't remember our guest.

Imagine if we had that ability to share the realities of all the species we share our planet with? Would we still hunt or catch or farm and eat them? Would we be more peaceful? Would we use it on each other?

The Bardo plays with a similar idea, kind of. Many religions believe that we are reincarnated after each life and death, that we are reborn in a new body, and live again. Each life is a chance to better ourselves, whether man or woman, brown or white. But what if all life was recycled on the planet? Who's to say who, or what, we (or even our pet dog) started out as? The Bardo is a concept from Tibetan Buddhism, a place in between life and rebirth. The story also takes a little of my own thinking about the earth as an organic whole, a place with a life force, or a pulse. Lub-dub, lub-dub. Is life the 'lub' and death the 'dub'? Is death the space in between, or is life? Whatever it is, the force that animates all life on the planet animates us, and maybe that force, to stick with this imagery, is the blood being pumped. Taan becomes captured by that life force and becomes a part of it, circulated through incarnations. As, perhaps, we all are.

Whether it is metaphor or real, ideas like the Bardo and reincarnation can encourage compassion and understanding. How can I hate that person? She may have been my mother in a past life! How could I be racist? I just happen to be born a certain colour this time. In my previous lives, I was probably all the other colours or shades of skin under the sun. Maybe, lifetimes ago, we were Taan, and travelled across the galaxy, but our ship got trapped in the pull of life on this beautiful planet. Maybe we were a mouse, or a bird. The idea deserves more words than I gave it in this story, but it is a start. I wrote the story years ago, on paper, which was lost or accidentally thrown away. It may have been longer, but the size fits. Would more animals add to the description, or just belabour the point?

But to explore another concept a bit further. I mentioned above the idea of the earth as an organic whole, a pulsing orb of life. I recently watched a sea anemone on a television program and will put that image on the table. An anemone is a predator, but let's forget that side of it for a moment. It's not what it is, but how it does it. It has arms of a sort that wave above it, waiting for prey to get close, to touch the arms. Once touched, the prey becomes stuck and pulled. Now imagine a sphere, that orb of life, with arms all around it, reaching out for other form of life. Or gentle fingers, trying to touch. Taan touched one of those and was brought down into the wholeness of life on Earth. I'm not really satisfied with that image, but it kind of works. The predatory nature in the analogy might be worth exploring in another, darker story.

The Originals comes from the body of *Seeders* (my second science fiction novel), and I'm being cheeky converting it to story form here, but after a year of pandemic I couldn't resist. I actually wrote that chapter before we knew the word, *COVID*. As part of that story, I looked up death rates in some of humanity's worst pandemics. In the Black Plague nearly one third of Europeans died. That is unimaginable. We're aghast now at one or two percent. Imagine a pandemic with a one hundred percent fatality rate. Or don't. It's not a pleasant thought.

Second Seed is itself a seed for a third novel in that series. Just like with *Stepping Out*, I envisioned a prologue, of sorts, or a Part One of a much longer story. In *The Originals*, Arnil tells of her experience fleeing the planet Ruanae. In *Second Seed*, Laant is on the only other ship, the second seed ship, which is the last one to leave. Evacuations are never tidy, just as I imagine theirs wasn't. Someone has to decide when to seal the doors and admit no others, condemning all those outside to death. Laant was not the one who made that decision, but he had to enforce it. Does that make him guilty? Did he even have a choice? And why focus on the choice, or even the act, when ultimately there may not have been a choice at all. If there were infected on the refugee ship, and that was introduced to the seed ship, much, much more would be lost. Sentimentality could cost all their lives. But to save their Ruan-ity, they had to sacrifice their Ruan-ness. That would have to have an impact on the type of civilisation they eventually create if they find a habitable world. I should know. The rough plan I have is that it does, with some dire consequences once they get a hold of that Donut technology sometime in the future.

A Little Night Action I owe to a FOS (Fisheries' Observer Supervisor). The FOS make all the arrangements for the observer, from the vessel they'll board, to helping them pay for the taxi to the port. I was delighted on a recent pass through the office to pick up my gear and briefing instructions to find out that most of the FOS are science fiction fans. Our conversations were like water to a thirsty man. Susannah, the FOS for my training trip, told me she had an idea. Imagine a mechanical fish that you could control, she said, that was able to swim with schools of fish. "You can have that," she added. "It can be in a story." I was over a thousand kilometers away at sea, and well out sight of land, before I found a use for Susannah's fish. Although, I'm not sure she envisioned it being used as it was in the hands of the Fish Liberation Front, or whoever they were. I emailed the story to her from the computer in the bridge while we were somewhere in the Southern Ocean fishing for squid. I feel like I should probably apologise for mis-using it. But instead, I'll say: "Thanks for the fish."

Twisted Love contains my first explicit sex scene ever committed to paper. In this collection, it's positioned after *Landing Party*, which I wrote later and maybe got a bit carried away. I killed them, after all. I have a friend who delights in the erotic in her story, a writer of crime and romance, and I know she would call me tame. I have had sex in a story before writing the scene in *Twisted Love*, but always kept it under the covers. I read in one book on writing that the most powerful sex scene ever written was in *Gone with the Wind*. Rex carries Scarlet up the stairs. End of sex scene. It is powerful because it is all implied. Yeah, I get it. But some sex just has to be more explicit. It's fun that way (and sex should be fun), and it shows us a lot about this alien. What she is practicing is similar to what is known as Tantric sex, using the powerful energies created during lovemaking. That's what something was feeding off in *Landing Party*.

She's intriguing, this alien. I want to know more about her!

Twisted Love is not a story about sex, or necessarily about love. Rather, it's about time. It's a vehicle for me to explore an idea. With distances being so great in this galaxy, timing seems to be quite a lottery. I played with this in *Earth Story*. Maybe the Earth was visited millions of years ago, even colonised. We missed it, because we weren't around. Bad luck, huh? Or bad timing. It seems the only way we could actually make contact with a sentient species is having an idea of *when* they were, not just where, and then being able to twist or corkscrew time as we fold space to make sure we bump into each other. Say we do receive a transmission, travelling at the speed of light. Chances are, even if we could get to the source, the senders would be hundreds or thousands of years gone. Lightspeed is usually considered extremely fast. Over one hundred and eighty thousand miles per second! But the distances between stars makes that seem like a crawl. Our own transmissions are making their way across the galaxy right now. Television is quiet young. Are those transmissions now sixty or seventy lightyears away? Maybe in a thousand years somebody, somewhere, will hear it and come visit in response. Too bad we missed them.

Folding not only space, but also time, is a concept I would like to explore more. Short story allows the writer to skip a lot, and leave a lot unanswered. It's just a snap shot, after all. But there's a lot to build on here, I think. What was the transmission we received? What was the mission to respond to it? Who was our main character, the human? Who was the alien woman? What were these powers of attraction? What happened to the concurrent mission? How could a love like that play out, when one would have to sacrifice so much in order for it to bloom? I don't want to say, 'stay tuned,' because that would sound too much like a promise. But ... we'll see.

On my training voyage as a fisheries observer, I thought I would be sharing a cabin. After four weeks initial training on land, new observers go on a five-to-six-week trip to really learn what's involved. I thought sharing a cabin would be a great way to collect conversation. What I had in mind was a snap shot of life in deep space, of two guys sharing a cabin for months on end in the middle of the big nowhere. A deep-sea fishing vessel is a bit like a space ship, after all. Crew are confined to the ship, a small enclosed water tight thing in the middle of a whole bunch of water.

Instead, I showed up to the boat with my trainer, a very experienced observer, to find out that we had our own cabins. Mine was actually very comfortable, with a shower and toilet, an L shaped couch, a television, and my bunk. There was enough room in the cabin to do yoga. Well, at least some stretches. So, the idea behind *Bunk Mate* changed to fit circumstance. Instead of two characters, it had one. We steamed for two whole days. That's what it's called when the boat goes a long distance. I don't know why it's still called that—these old terms stick around for a long, long time. It sounds better than 'dieseling', which is probably more accurate. Anyway, I was basically in my cabin for hours. That's nothing compared to what our character went through, his months and months alone in space, and like I said, my cabin was very comfortable. But it is when I wrote the story.

Further Books

Read all of the *Lucid* series from Dreaming Big
Publications (*American Dreamer, Tomorrow's
History* and *Gods and Dreamers*)

Check out science fiction coming soon!

To learn more about Christopher's books, visit him
at:

www.christophermcmaster.com

American Dreamer

Can one person change a reality?

Chicago. 1944. Waking in a dream Nadia finds herself in a class with two other students. The woman posing as their teacher (if indeed she is a woman) breaks each of them with terrifying nightmares, and 'tasks' to complete while awake, that destroys any hope of escape.

But Nadia begins to realise she isn't quite alone, not exactly powerless, and that there are those besides Miss Biel who want a certain outcome. There comes a time when she has to decide who to trust.

American Dreamer weaves present and past in a narrative that transports the reader to an earlier age, and slowly wakes them to an alternative reality, not too distant than our own present.

"A great story, imaginative and absorbing. I read the whole book over a weekend, couldn't put it down. The crossing between alternate universes and parallel lives was like American Gods written by Neil Gaiman. It was a reminder that even in these troubled times, things could be worse!"

—Amazon reviewer

Tomorrow's History

Can one person save a reality?

London. Present day. Sunlight glints off solar panels, harvesting the energy that keeps the city moving. Roof gardens add a hint of green to the skyline. Airships pass overhead on their way north to the capital, Jorvik. Ships of the Great Fleet load at the busy docks, preparing for the voyage across the Western Ocean to the Far Settlements, holding the Norse world together.

Jakob thinks his world is safe. But it isn't. Something needs finishing for his present to come to pass, and for some unknown reason he has been chosen to do it. Trapped in his dreams, and thrust into an age of Vikings who are much more familiar with the sword and the axe, he uses the only thing he has—his wits.

Tasked with leading a party of Danes in pursuit of royal game, he is swept into an adventure that can only have one outcome if Britain, and the Danelaw, is to survive.

Gods and Dreamers

Time kills all things. Even the gods.

We all dream. Only most of don't remember. How can we even know what we do in our dreams if the memory fades like mist when we wake up? Teeny, Robbie, and Thieu start to recall their dreams and the disturbing acts of violence and servitude that they are coerced into committing in timelines other than theirs.

Awareness breeds rebellion. Led by Petrit and Nadia, who enlist the new rebels into their secret campaign against the manipulative gods, the dreamers learn how to use their lucidity to resist the oppressive forces that control their dreams and realities alike. Together, the dreamers struggle to protect their timelines and push back against the gods that exploit mortals for entertainment and rewrite human history for their sustained nourishment.

But first they have to survive. There are others who think them heretics and will try to stop them at all costs.

Pirates Come Down

Fishing in the near future takes more than a net!

Rickets is a PAC-Man, his patrol and attack craft the first line of defense against encroaching vessels. Moss is a Fisheries Observer, tasked with ensuring companies follow the rules set for target species. Together they play a part in ensuring the waters are not fished to extinction.

But as fisheries elsewhere are wiped out, New Zealand waters start to look more attractive until every ship protects itself with PAC boats, missiles that skim the surface, and kamikaze drones equipped with explosives.

Only there is a bigger shadow on the horizon, one that deflects all radar, is lethally armed, and takes what it wants!

MisStep

Science fiction coming soon:

Jens needed to get off the planet in a hurry so he took the first job on an interstellar freighter he found—part of a convoy to a far-flung mining colony, three Steps and almost three thousand lightyears away. Only the desperate went so far—colonists willing to trade a life on Earth for a new start on a rock somewhere across the galaxy, or spacers one step ahead of the law.

But as each Step takes him farther from home, Jens learns that the job isn't exactly what he was told, the cargo not as legitimate, and his situation even more precarious. Jens finds himself being groomed for a role in an interplanetary drug racket, with no way out.

Then the convoy mis-Steps, emerging lightyears off course, and the miscalculation might not be their fault!

Seeders

The exciting sequel to MisStep:

They tried to hide from certain death. Now it's time to find them.

A pandemic spread over their planet and swept them from history. In a desperate act to save their species they launched a remnant of survivors into the depths of space, frozen in cryo-sleep, to be awakened only when their ship detected a habitable planet. But there were no planets and the ship continued into the cold and dark.

Thousands of years later humans have settled the ocean world. Picking through the ruins of what was once a mighty civilization, xeno-linguist Peter Taylor and a small research team find evidence of the Original's desperate mission. Plotting the probable course of the ship, the team locate where it might be, if it really exists, and if it is still operational.

The promised technology of the Originals outweighs any 'ifs'. But they need the help of a powerful earth-based consortia, as well as from Andrew Jensen, the only man to ever survive a confrontation with those whose planet they now call their own.

www.christophermcmaster.com

Printed in Great Britain
by Amazon

33418929R10138